POISON FLOWERS

by

Nat Burns

Bella
BOOKS

2013

Copyright © 2013 by Nat Burns

Bella Books, Inc.
P.O. Box 10543
Tallahassee, FL 32302

All rights reserved. No part of this book may be reproduced or transmitted in any form or by any means, electronic or mechanical, including photocopying, without permission in writing from the publisher.

Printed in the United States of America on acid-free paper
First published 2013

Editor: Medora MacDougall
Cover Designer: Judy Fellows

ISBN 13: 978-1-59493-321-9

PUBLISHER'S NOTE
The scanning, uploading, and distribution of this book via the Internet or via any other means without the permission of the publisher is illegal and punishable by law. Please purchase only authorized electronic editions, and do not participate in or encourage electronic piracy of copyrighted materials. Your support of the author's rights is appreciated.

Other Bella Books by Nat Burns

Two Weeks in August
House of Cards
Identity
Quality of Blue, The
Book of Eleanor, The

Dedication

I'd like to dedicate this book to my two daughters, Jessica and Rachel, who, even when very small, showed infinite patience as they waited for mom to scribble yet one more story.

Acknowledgment

Many thanks to Bella Books, my home away from home, and to my sweet editor, Medora MacDougall. What would I do without her calm advice? Also thanks to those friends who pre-read *Poison Flowers* and shared their advice and approval. It was much appreciated.

About the Author

Nat Burns lives in beautiful Albuquerque, New Mexico, truly the Land of Enchantment, where she writes full time, helped by a houseful of cats. *www.natburns.com*

CHAPTER ONE

"Hey, baby, what you doing out here all by yourself?"

The young man appeared before her with such abruptness that she gasped and choked, breaking into a spasm of coughing. She held up one hand, gesturing for him to wait as she struggled for control. The youth, no older than seventeen certainly, turned to his handful of friends and snickered at her predicament. They responded with muffled laughter.

Eyeing them as she tried to still her spasming throat, Marya knew a moment of fear. She had an open mind, always had. She truly believed in freedom of expression. Yet she also knew the dangers arising from substance abuse and irresponsible young people. It wasn't the group's abundance of tattoos and piercings that alarmed her nor their choices of black leather as accouterments. It was the challenge of their eyes as they watched her. She could see them making judgments: How much harm would come to them if they harmed her?

Marya wished suddenly that she had driven away upon first spying the then-distant quartet of young people. They had been strolling carelessly along the edge of the sand and loudly whooping out their indignation at being baptized by the ever-moving waves. Their rowdy behavior should have been a clear indicator that she didn't want to be alone in their company.

"Hey, is that your Trooper up there?" asked a young girl, her bleached hair colored bright pink on one side, baby blue on the other. "How 'bout you take us for a ride? Ricky, make her take us for a ride."

She watched Marya intently, pale blue eyes heavily outlined in black kohl and mascara. The other girl in the group, thinner, with long blond hair blowing across her face, watched her as well.

"Yeah," chimed in a young boy who had a fine silver chain running from his nose to his ear. "We wanna go into the strip. You take us, lady?"

"No, I'm sorry," Marya choked out finally. "I have someone waiting for me. I've got to get there as soon as I can."

"Is it a boyfriend, *señorita*?" This was asked by Ricky, the first one who had spoken, the one she immediately recognized as the ringleader.

"That's none of your business," she said as she rose to her feet. She patted sand from her hands and started to move away.

"Hey wait, lady, you got sand all over you!" The two boys descended on her and began playfully slapping sand from her bottom and legs as they circled around her, shouting encouragement to one another. The girls watched and shouted suggestions.

"Look here, you two!" Marya said loudly as she stilled and stood her ground. "I want you to stop this right now."

"Or what, sweet thing? I'll tell you what, you gonna give us a ride into Myrtle Beach, that's what."

Ricky moved close, too close for her to be comfortable, and she, without even thinking about it, crouched into defensive mode, calling upon her years of taekwondo training. But before she needed to defend herself, a spate of rocks came whistling out of the sky. One struck the chain-faced boy on his shoulder; he yelped as the group turned to face the attacker. To her surprise, it was a short, stocky woman. She stood barefoot on the beach, her light cotton pants rolled to her knees and a loose button-down shirt billowing in the ocean wind. Her hair, cropped close, appeared pure white and actually gleamed in the slanting sunlight.

"Oh shit! It's her!" one girl blurted in a *sotto voce* exclamation.

"I see her," said the ringleader in a harsh, disparaging mutter. Another rock sailed toward them, so quickly that Marya didn't even see the woman move. It found its mark, on the ringleader's thigh, and he growled as he clasped his leg in both hands. He glared at the woman.

"Get on with you," the woman called, her voice low and bearing an undeniable ring of authority. "I'll not have you on my property. I've told you that too many times. I'm getting tired of repeating myself."

Silence fell as the ruffians mulled over the implied threat. Finally, cowed and with much impotent glowering and muttering, they moved as one unit up the beach in the direction from which they'd come.

Marya breathed a sigh of relief and relaxed her posture. Impulsively, she rushed toward the woman and threw her arms around her shoulders in a quick hug of gratitude.

"Thank you, thank you," she said. "I was beginning to get worried."

This close, Marya could see the woman's face. She realized she was older than she was by more than a decade and was handsome, with smooth, defined features and striking blue eyes. Suddenly feeling foolish, she stepped back, hands twitching nervously at her sides.

"Aren't you going to say something?" she asked after many moments of silence had passed.

"You should be worried," the woman said in a hard, pedantic tone. "I can't believe you were stupid enough to be out here alone, with evening coming on. I particularly resent you adding to the trouble I already have with these kids."

She looked Marya over with mistrustful, dismissing eyes. "You're not much above a brat yourself, are you? Get on off my property, or I'll call the cops and have *your* ass hauled in."

With that comment, she turned and walked away from Marya, her strong legs and feet churning sand.

Bewildered and unbelievably hurt by the stranger's irritation, anger stirred in Marya. She had never been what one would call coolheaded and suddenly she was seeing red. And, of course, her mouth shot off, taking on a life of its own.

"Could we *be* any bitchier?" she called after the woman. "You're just damned lucky those kids didn't decide to gang up on your ass. One day those rocks won't cut it anymore and then what will you do?"

Her rescuer ignored her, mounting the wooden porch steps that led to the interesting house that had drawn Marya into this little drama. Marya made her way up the sloping, grassy hill toward her car.

"I hope your damned house falls off into the ocean," she muttered, just for good measure.

She turned once at the top and studied the scene below. The road offered a wide green shoulder before sloping into a scenic expanse of tan sand and dusky blue ocean. The large house just past this stretch of beach angled away from the sea and its appearance had snared her interest as she drove by. The house was crisp white against the cobalt of the water, a two-story Cape Cod with a wide, wooden porch that jutted out over the ocean. It was an unusual style for this area. Yet whoever built the house had planned wisely, for although the house site appeared to be centuries old—judging from the amount of seashore that had eroded from around it—the solid home rested sturdy on a dais of huge stones, some naturally occurring, others appearing to have been laid like puzzle pieces and mortared together.

Earlier, guiding her car over a sloping dune, Marya had pulled onto the grassy expanse that demarcated the beach from the highway and sat a moment savoring the sound of waves coming ashore. Eventually lulled into obedience to the water's call, she had left the car and meandered across the sand, further drawn in by a lavender banner atop a flagpole that snapped with high energy in the ocean wind. It drew her attention for it appeared a statement, mounted as it was in an offshore rocky formation. Though she had walked as close to the water as it was possible to do without sacrificing her sandals, she saw no indication of what it signified.

"Probably a landmark for boats, so they'll stay away from her," she told herself now as she laid one hand on the hood of her car, preparatory to leaving.

Dim lights had brought several of the house windows to life, and she caught a glimpse of the white-haired woman as she passed by just inside one of them. Who was she? And why did she seem to hate people so much? More importantly, why did she seem to hate *her*?

CHAPTER TWO

The girl had been feisty. Dorry could appreciate that. She watched through the window as the redhead mounted the grassy dune separating Dundun Beach from the highway, noting how her lithe form made her appear to float above the flora.

Though she was small, her arms had been strong when they hugged Dorry close.

Dorry took in a deep breath, reliving, for a brief moment, how that embrace had affected her. It had been such a long time since anyone had held her. As if facing death, she had, in that moment, seen her life flash before her eyes and realized how solitary she had allowed it to become. She closed her eyes and savored anew the memory of a soft, slightly rounded body pressed to hers. Her thoughts flew to other embraces, long ago, from a body even more full, more voluptuous. A body that smelled like the Far East from a rich, heady perfume. A body that she had loved to distraction.

Dorry turned from the window and studied the living room of her home. She enjoyed the monotone simplicity of this room, the richness of the brown on brown. The wood of the walls and floor had been salvaged from shipwrecks and polished to a smooth sheen by her paternal great-grandfather. He'd been a sailor and had built this home so his wife and six children could watch as he passed by on his way to Begaman Harbor, some thirty nautical miles north, when he was scheduled to come home. Those were big days in the Wood household. Grandma Ashton had beamed with joy as she told young Dorry about his homecomings when she was a girl. He was always laden with presents for his children, and their mother had always prepared a feast of good food to celebrate the event.

Dorry walked to the long wooden bar that defined the eastern wall and poured a healthy two fingers of single-malt scotch. She carried it to the window and looked out at the traffic passing by on Route 17.

They were all dead now. Her great-grandparents, grandparents and even parents. And now her only sister, taken by cancer two years ago. Dorry was truly alone, the last of her line.

Alone.

Old memories rose and conquered her. Memories of the woman she had loved so fiercely. Tears filled her eyes and then ran with frenzied haste down her cheeks. She didn't bother to wipe them away. Her thoughts had drifted to joining her family. She could see herself walking along a white tunnel toward them. She saw her father's jolly smile as he welcomed her. Her mother's open arms, which would give her solace from all of life's demands. She could be free from the guilt and sadness that defined her life these days. It would be such an easy thing to give up…to go join them all and become a trusting child again.

"Ahhh, fuck no," she said loudly. She scrubbed at her face with one hand as her other lifted the scotch to her lips. She drained the glass, welcoming the liquid heat as it burned her throat and blazed a noticeable path to her stomach. She was alive and kicking, and she would continue that way, thank you very much.

Her gaze drifted toward where she had last seen the feisty redhead. She remembered everything about her. Was she a tourist? Had to be, or Dorry would know of her. Damn, but she had been pretty with those huge blue eyes and that gorgeous auburn hair. Dorry had always been a sucker for freckled redheads.

She smiled as she let her imagination roam free. She could see them having coffee together after a night of passion…their gazes would meet and they would smile. Dorry started physically as another face appeared. A dear, beloved face that was lost to her now.

She growled and moved to the bar where she slammed down the glass. It just wasn't fair. Life wasn't fair.

She fished her cell phone from her pocket and called the one friend she had left. As she did most evenings.

His voice on the other end of the line calmed her immediately and she knew again why she was alive and healthy. Why she persevered. It was for and because of him. He'd lost Dolly too, and he knew alone just as well as Dorry did.

"Have you had dinner?" he asked, his gentle voice scolding; he knew she hadn't eaten.

Dorry laughed, and, carrying her friend's voice with her, she moved down the long hall toward the kitchen.

CHAPTER THREE

The old codger sidled up to the counter and, with a grunt, settled onto the stool next to her. She wasn't worried; she knew the type. Widower at loose ends. A somewhat annoying bearer of local lore. Leaning forward, she blew on her coffee and took a cautious sip.

"Hello there, young 'un," he said as he perused the menu.

"Hello, yourself. You doing all right this evening?" She studied him, her reporter mind filing away a description of his appearance: thick, short salt-and-pepper hair—more salt than pepper—a deeply lined, tanned face with perpetually squinting brown eyes and heavy, drooping lips. A typical middle-aged, paunchy body. He wore belted, low-slung jeans and a button-down western-style shirt.

His grin showed relief and she saw some of his habitual loneliness ease up. "I'm finer than frog hair in the dead of summer," he replied jovially.

She was procrastinating, putting off her arrival at her parents' house, and the Fetch It Diner was doing a good job of providing just the diversion she needed. And more time to ponder the latest burning question: Why did coming home this way feel so much like failing? Here she was, thirty years old, old enough to be on her own and taking care of herself, back with her parents again.

"You having the usual, Kent?" the waitress asked. She waited expectantly on the other side of the counter. Her tired air had weighed her down until her body had spun itself into a snug cocoon of indifference.

"Yeah, Lisa, sounds good," he replied.

She hurried off and silence slammed heavy between them.

"Marya Brock," she said, extending her hand.

He took it in his callused paw. "Kent Sayers."

"So, Kent, you a native?"

"Yeah, I am. Born and raised just down the street a ways. I'm on my way out of town, though," he said, adding a steady stream of sugar to the coffee Lisa slid in front of him. "I truck for Ferguson."

"Ahh." Marya nodded slowly. Ferguson handled a large nationwide fleet of eighteen-wheelers. "Where you heading?"

"Up 95. Maine, believe it or not. Got a load of Florida cypress I brung up yesterday."

She gave a low whistle. "Man, someone paid for that."

He laughed, the sound a low tone, throttled in his throat. "You got that right. It's that pecky wood too, and that's dear to everyone."

He sipped his coffee and sighed contentedly. "You from here?"

"Nope, Seattle."

"Washington State? Now that's a long haul. What brings you to the East Coast?"

She hesitated. She wasn't about to come out to this stranger, figuring the world he lived in wouldn't even allow him to grasp the idea of a lesbian relationship, much less how painfully one could end.

"Just needed a change, I guess," she said finally. "My parents live here."

"Over in Florence?"

"Oh no, here, in Marstown. Schuyler Point," she amended.

He smiled. "You know why they call it Marstown?"

She grinned inside. She had pegged him correctly. Local lore. "No, why?"

Marya already knew the people of eastern South Carolina had always called the small coastal village Marstown, even though its real name—the one on all the maps—was Schuyler Point. She didn't fess up to any knowledge, though, letting him tell her the whole story. About how no one remembered exactly why it was called Marstown, but it was said it had something to do with the strange red rocks that periodically washed up on some of the beaches. No one could explain the flaky red shards of stone, but there had been several articles published over the years that attributed it to a deep ocean trench just offshore that was full of volcanic residue. It had always seemed plausible to her and Kent obviously concurred.

"And then there's some that say they call it Marstown because Martians been seen in the water off Begaman Cove," he added, piquing her interest.

She leaned back, shifting her weight. She had been listening to him absently, watching him, her chin cupped in one palm. "Martians."

He eyed her, eyes twinkling. "Martians. In little red spaceships."

Lisa slid an oval-shaped, steaming platter full of burger, french fries and sunny-side up eggs in front of him. He unwrapped his set-up and looked at the empty spot on the counter before Marya. "Not eating?"

"I know," she said, nodding in agreement. "Too skinny. I just have a high metabolism. Believe me; I've been stuffing my face all the way across the country, with a carload of snacks you wouldn't believe." She indicated the coffee cup that Lisa was refilling. "Just needed a wake up."

Kent nodded and dug in. Half a fried egg and a quarter of the burger disappeared before he spoke again. "What's your field, Marya? You got a job here?"

"Not at the moment. I'm a journalist, though, a writer. I'm hoping to find work in Myrtle Beach, but if not, I'll just wait tables until I find a reporter job."

Kent nodded as he chewed. "Yeah, anyone can do that... for a while," he said.

They both looked at Lisa simultaneously. She was standing off to one side, flipping through a garish tabloid.

"No offense," he muttered.

"None taken," she replied, setting the magazine aside and leaning in to top off his coffee cup.

"So, reporter, huh? I bet you've seen it all," Kent continued.

"Oh, enough. People never fail to amaze and amuse me."

And Kent was off, telling Marya story after interesting story, each one more comical than the last. Lisa joined in on the ones she remembered and laughter rang in the tiny, mostly deserted diner. Marya stayed and listened, even though it was getting late and she should have been moseying on to her parents' house. But, after all, this is why she became a journalist; she enjoyed people's stories. But soon afternoon turned into early evening and Kent finally seemed to be talked out.

"Well," he said, balling up his paper napkin and tossing it into his empty plate. "Guess I'd better be moving on. That road doesn't get any shorter the longer I wait."

Marya nodded and rose, stretching stiff legs and arms. "Some say it gets longer," she offered.

Kent laughed and stood. "Some would say that and it might be the truth. Listen, young 'un. You be safe out there, and I hope you have real good luck while you're in Marstown."

She took his hand, shaking it firmly in farewell. "Thanks for the stories, Kent. You made my day. Drive carefully on that long road, you hear?"

She stood and watched his huge silver truck roar past her SUV before getting into it. Minutes later she reached the Braxton Hills subdivision where her parents now lived. Two blocks further and she arrived at their modest, ranch-style brick home, which she had only visited once before. She was surprised that she remembered all the convoluted turns through their subdivision.

She parked in the driveway, pulling her car in next to their white Lincoln, switched off the engine and the lights and took a deep breath. Then her mother was there, hugging her close. She began to feel better immediately. The bosom of the family was just that, she thought, our first place of nurture. This was home, the beginning and the end.

CHAPTER FOUR

"There's just no hope for it," Mama said as she peered through the front picture window. It directed her gaze out into an empty suburban street, but I knew that wasn't what Mama was seeing. She saw old betrayal and lies looking back at her.

"What do you mean?" I asked slowly. When Mama got that faraway look, I knew trouble was afoot. I studied her pale, carefully curled hair and wondered about the drama of her day. I guess she had tried to get money again. I sort of wished she'd give it up. We seemed to be doing okay and every time she went through this, it...changed her a little. That scared me.

"The bitch said no again. Said you were too full-growed for help. Didn't matter about college, nothing," she added, turning to study me with weighing eyes. "Like you look growed."

I looked down at my arms and legs. They looked fine to me. I knew I was powerful even though she would never see it. The baggy jeans I was wearing didn't help, I guess.

"It's not bad, Mama. I'm getting stronger."

"No thanks to that battle-ax, you ain't."

Her tone softened. "Go on, honey. I left you some hot food in the kitchen. Eat up, now. You just let Mama handle that cursed family of yours."

I leaned to kiss her cheek and I smelled the lemony perfume that defined her for me. She always smelled the same, had ever since I was a kid. I had learned one thing in my secretive, sorry life. I could always depend on Mama.

"Imagine the nerve of her, full of secrets and lies but still making out like she's the high-and-mighty queen over everyone. I hate her so much," she said softly, her eyes gazing at stuff I couldn't see.

I left the room, taking care to be very quiet. It was always better, when she got like this, just to disappear for a while.

CHAPTER FIVE

"I called the receptionist over at the *Times*, and she wants you to come in first thing Monday to meet with the editor, Ed Bush. You got here at just the right time; one of their reporters moved away this past week."

Marya's mother dumped a second spoonful of sugar into her tea, stirred it, then took a cautious sip. She was sitting across the table from Marya in her warm, welcoming kitchen.

Marya's tea was Earl Grey. She let the rich aroma of the brew wash across her before she ruined the anticipation with a first sip. A discarded copy of the *Schuyler Times* lay on a nearby counter. She fetched it.

"What's he like?" she asked, perusing the paper with a practiced eye. It was very much like the small-town papers she had worked on for the past ten years. She knew exactly how it was put together.

"Who? Ed? He's okay, I suppose. Seems to have a good sense of humor."

She lifted her eyes and studied her mother, feeling as though she were looking into a slightly distorted mirror. They both had the same short, copper-colored hair, although her mother's was straight and hers naturally curled. They also shared the same dark blue eyes and pale, freckled skin. She was thinner than her mother, however, not able to shake her teenaged lankiness.

"How did you meet him?" she asked, wondering suddenly what her parents' day-to-day life was like.

Her mother laughed, surprising her. "A dog," she said, then added in explanation, "This little terrier appeared one day at our back door and just stayed and stayed. I felt so sorry for it. I fed him and washed him and tried to talk him into going home but he seemed totally lost. So, after a day or so, I went down to the newspaper office to put a classified ad in the lost and found section. I'm glad I did because the owner, a sweet little old lady, had been frantic. She saw the ad as soon as the paper came out and called me. The reunion of those two was incredible. I wish I could have videotaped it."

"So, what? This Ed Bush took the ad?" Her mother hadn't really answered the question.

"Well, actually, it was funny. Your father was with me, and though Ed started taking the ad, he and your dad started talking about fishing and that was that. I bet it took us two hours before we got out of there. He's a real friendly guy."

Marya chuckled and took a deep sip of her tea. "I hope he's a good boss. That's all I care about."

Her mother shrugged. "It is my understanding the other reporter left because he wanted to move inland, not because the job was bad."

Marya nodded to show she understood. "Where is Dad, by the way?"

She laughed. "Deep sea fishing, where else? He's developed a full-blown passion for it."

A vision of her father wrestling a huge swordfish filled Marya's mind and she had to grin. Her thin, bookish father was not what one would call the athletic type. Her mother saw her grin and seemed to understand the reason for it.

"Oh, most of it is throwing in the line long enough to get sunburned and then drinking beer with his buddies over at Randy's pub after dark. He doesn't struggle too hard."

They laughed together and fell into a companionable silence. Her mother rose and fetched another cup of tea, mint this time; Marya could tell by the faint aroma that carried to her as her mother reclaimed her seat.

"Do you want to talk about it?" Her mother watched her with sad eyes, her mouth pressed into a tight line.

Hating the fact that she had helped cause the faint worry lines now marring that dear, familiar face, Marya had a sudden revelation about the responsibilities of parenting. She wondered if she would ever feel ready for such a monumental task. She sighed, trying to bring her mind back to the question.

"There's not so much to tell, Mom. We just weren't getting along. She started seeing other people. That's all. It happens all the time."

Her mother studied her. "Tell me this, Marya. What is it you want from a relationship?"

She thought about the unexpected question. "I don't know. I want someone who gets me, I guess. And a meeting of the minds, the soul. Most of the people I've been with can't see beyond their own noses, don't understand that there's a bigger picture out there." She paused a handful of seconds before continuing.

"And then there's chemistry. I want to have intense chemistry with someone. I also need a certain amount of touching, close physical contact. I feel lost when I'm not touched a lot in a relationship."

"Do you mean sex? What?"

Marya blushed. "Sure, that too, but I need other stuff as well—kissing, cuddling, you know. There's a certain level of intimacy that I can't find...and really can't seem to achieve even in myself when relating to others. I suppose it's actually a matter of trusting someone."

Her mom nodded acceptance, and after a moment, Marya continued.

"Did you ever see the movie *Touching Hearts*?"

Her mother shook her head and leaned in to sip her tea.

"I guess you haven't." Marya laughed with some embarrassment. "It's made more for people like me. But it's about these two women who fall in love. I don't need to tell you the whole story because it was the scenes of the women together that touched me. I dreamed about it for days afterward. Their need spoke to me, they really needed one another in so many ways. Their closeness was incredible."

She broke off. How could she express in words the deep feelings the movie had spawned in her? She looked at her mother helplessly. Luckily, she seemed to understand.

"You mean there was an unusual tenderness between the two of them and that's what you'd like to have."

Marya nodded slowly, doubtfully, knowing it was not as simple as that.

Her mother took a deep breath and leaned back in her chair. "Well, I think we all want that at one time or another, especially when we're young. But as time passes..."

"As time passes, what?" Marya asked dully after many moments had passed.

"We grow up and realize that romance books or movies are the only places where such tenderness and love exist."

She raised her gaze to Marya's. "I'm sorry, honey. Other things grow in importance, such as building a family and careers. Most women get what they need from their children, others from closeness with their women friends."

Doubt washed over Marya. Had she subconsciously, or even consciously, allowed her relationship with Kim to end because of an impossible dream? No. Thinking of her split with Kim always brought a certain amount of regret, but deep inside she knew she'd made the right decision. But her mother, had *she* given up? Settled for less?

"I can't believe that, Mom. I know it's out there and I can find it. The right person just needs to come along, that's all."

Her mother nodded. "I can't find fault with what happened between you and Kim. I hope this will be another chance for you."

Marya knew what she meant without her spelling it out. She wanted Marya to try dating men again as she had in high school.

"It's still early," she replied, trying to lighten her deliberate sidestep, "but I feel happier already. I mean, look, I'm in the process of moving to a new town, and day after tomorrow I'm going to see your Mr. Bush and knock this town back on its heels with my writing panache."

"Confident cuss," her mother muttered, standing. "Let's see about unpacking your car. Do you still have your Asian antimaterialism fetish?"

Marya laughed at the novel terminology as she joined her. "Yep, all my worldly possessions are packed into six large boxes. I tried for five, but my books kept interfering."

"Oh." Her mother stopped so suddenly that Marya bumped into her back, almost shoving her through the kitchen door and into the cool, ocean-brushed evening outside. "I checked around about your classes. There are two karate houses out on the main road in Myrtle Beach, but I'm warning you, they're probably pretty expensive and I wouldn't trust some of those guys as far as I could throw them. Know what I mean?"

Marya nodded and they resumed their journey outside. "Instructors concerned only with the tournament circuit and what trophies they can bring home, right?"

"Absolutely. Not to mention the fact that one of them looks like an Elvis Presley clone."

Marya laughed and opened the door on the driver's side.

"There is one alternative, though."

Marya stilled and peered at her mother, concerned by her tone.

"There is an actual taekwondo class here in Marstown," she said slowly.

"Okay, what's wrong with it?"

She smiled a funny smile, one-half of her mouth tilted down in dislike. "Nothing so terrible. It's run by Dorcas Wood."

Marya lifted a box and maneuvered it, and her body, out from behind the Trooper's heavy door. "So, what's a Dorcas Wood?"

"She's an...unusual lady who lives over on the knoll. She seems nice enough, though she's something of a hermit."

"But she teaches the martial art, taekwondo, right?" Marya called this back over her shoulder as she moved inside with the box.

Her mother was close behind so she waited, holding the door for her.

The two moved silently along the long hallway that stretched off the kitchen. The guest room was at the end.

"Thanks for the great room, Mom," Marya said.

"Well, it's a little musty, but I've aired it for you. I think you'll be comfortable. You even have your own bathroom."

Marya nodded as she placed the box on the soft floral counterpane. "It's nice you letting me stay here. Are you sure I won't be putting you and Dad out?"

"You'll always have a home with us," her mother said with a genuine smile of fondness. Marya's heart swelled and sudden tears filled her eyes. She blinked them away and hurried back outside to get a second carton.

"So which is the lesser of two evils then, in your opinion," she asked as they met at the car. "Should I go with the Elvis guy or this weird woman?"

"The images you conjure in someone's head," her mother replied with a low laugh. "I guess Miss Wood is about as good as any. She's cheaper, only sixty a month, and close by, here in town. What do *you* think?"

She struggled with a box of books.

"Here, I'll get that one. You get the striped one, over there. I don't know. She's probably pretty good. Women who go into martial arts have to be or they don't open their own schools. Is she a master?"

"Marya, I don't know about that stuff, you know that."

She disappeared inside the house. Marya lifted the box of books with difficulty but finally managed to swing the box onto one hip and shuffle it to the door. Her mom, arms now empty, held the door open for her.

"What are the hours like?" she queried when they met at the car for the final load. "Can I go anytime?"

Her mom nodded. "The cost covers unlimited access and she's open from six in the morning until eight at night."

Her mother held the door for her this time since the burden she was holding was smaller and less awkward.

"Okay, I'm sold. I'll sign up when I'm in town Monday. Now, what's for dinner, I'm hungry."

"Oh no, you're still a bottomless pit. Your father warned me, but I didn't believe him. I figured you had outgrown it," her mother said with a deep sigh.

"Mom! Me outgrow your wonderful stir-fry, your layered salad...your homemade apple pie? No way!"

Her mother set the box she carried on Marya's bed and reached to muss her hair. "It's good to have you home, pumpkin."

Marya pulled her mother into a full body hug. "It's good to be here."

CHAPTER SIX

Later that evening, finally alone, Marya stepped into a hot shower and let the grit from the road leave her body as she tried to relax and focus. Her thoughts proved uncooperative, however, and after getting soap in her eyes for the second time, she gave up, stilled and watched sudsy water flow into the drain as thoughts rushed through her.

Guilt had nagged at her periodically during the pleasant dinner of leftovers she had shared with her parents. What right had she to bring her unconventional self here and turn their lives upside down again?

Coming out to her parents when she was sixteen had been one of the most difficult moments of her life—and of theirs, she was beginning to understand. She had not realized until much later the long-term price she had asked them to pay, the dreams her announcement had shattered. There would be no grandchildren, no prideful recounting of romantic coups, no handsome, successful son-in-law to parade before their friends. Instead there was just the harsh reality of the nonchild, a daughter who existed but had to be spoken of circumspectly because of her very different lifestyle.

In her youthful bliss, Marya had seen their shock and their pain, but it did not diminish the excitement she had experienced in discovering who she was once and for all, in realizing she did not have to follow the paths of her peers. A newly formed gay and lesbian youth group at her high school helped her understand that it was okay to be the way she was, that she could love women the rest of her life if she so desired. The thought had made her giddy, banishing the self-doubt and self-abasement that had gone hand in hand with recognizing the differences between herself and other young women, heterosexual women, her own age.

By the time she went to college, however, she began to see that the lifestyle she had gleefully followed was fraught with perils, often more so than more conventional lifestyles. Hearing of lesbian sisters beaten and raped dampened some of her flamboyance and made her much more conservative in her mannerisms, even her attitudes. She was one of the lucky ones—she had never been physically attacked for her romantic choices—but as she set off into her career she realized that family friends had begun questioning her single status.

Her parents, of course, had been the ones forced to deal with the curious inquiries. When this awareness dawned on her one day, she was aghast, wondering how best to make things up to them. She couldn't find a way. All she could do was love them and accept the rare, unconditional love they eventually re-offered her. Not really a fair trade, all things considered.

Still, when she had happened upon an advertisement in a trade journal for a reporting job in Seattle, she leapt at the opportunity. Putting a continent between her parents and herself had seemed like a good idea then, a way to lead her own life without complicating theirs so much. Ten years later, she did not regret the move. What she did regret was allowing herself, in this moment of weakness, to come back into her parents' life and disrupt the beautiful retirement they'd set up for themselves.

Someone standing on the sidelines and observing their small family unit would probably think all was well. A daughter, though, could pick up the subtle nuances of her father's discomfort when her ex-lover was mentioned in passing, would notice the careful omission of inquiry into personal affairs.

Marya went into the bedroom and looked at her wet, bedraggled self in the mirror. Yes, the guilt was back and in spades. For their sake, she needed to find a place of her own and soon.

Besides, what would happen if she met someone new here in Marstown? She couldn't go back to those high school years when she had lived the lie of being the proper friend to girls she was attracted to. When she'd pulled her caressing hands from other girls although she'd wanted more. When she'd never kissed the soft lips she yearned for, quaking inside as she imagined how they would feel against hers.

She had lied to herself and others then because she had cherished the closeness of her family. An only child, born to her parents late in their lives, she had always depended on them, emotionally, physically, psychologically. This issue of lesbianism, this love of other women, had driven a wedge between them, but she couldn't lie anymore, couldn't deny the reality of who she was. Doing so just left her feeling shuttered, off balance.

Glancing at the clock, she pushed these introspective thoughts away and put herself into forward motion again. She prepared for bed, the thoughts beating inside her brain fluttering like the moth flapping helplessly on the other side of the window glass.

Things didn't get any better when she slipped into the guestroom's hard, seldom-used bed. Unable to sleep, she found herself reliving the traumatic moments that had changed her life and brought her back into her parents' home.

***

Kim's bags had been packed by the time she got home from the gym, she remembered. Placed neatly beside the front door, they fairly hummed with purposeful intent. She had closed the door and sighed, raking her eyes across the flawlessly matched suitcases. She despised the fact that the first thought that had invaded her mind was a hateful one: Whose arms were going to hold Kim tonight?

"Well, there you are. I was beginning to think I would have to leave without saying goodbye."

Kim stood in the doorway to the den, her lustrous black hair piled in unusual disarray. I allowed my gaze to travel across her one last time, filing away how her angular cheekbones accented her swarthy features, how her acute slimness gave her a certain air of elegance, of sleekness.

God, I was going to miss her.

"Marya, aren't you going to talk to me?" Kim poked her bottom lip out in that adorable pout I was far too familiar with.

"Yeah. Listen, I'm sorry about that fight this morning. I didn't mean what I said. I don't know what gets into me sometimes." The workout had mellowed my attitude and I was backtracking on my earlier ultimatum.

I lifted apologetic eyes. To my surprise, Kim smiled. A real smile too, from the old days. It was a big improvement over the pinched smirks I'd been getting the past few months.

"It's that damned Irish temper, is all," she explained, as if I knew nothing about it. "I'm all right. You don't have to fret about it."

I walked to the tall hall butler and removed my damp overcoat. I found it was easier to share my feelings with my back to her. "Well, I do fret. I never wanted this to happen, Kim."

There, the door had been opened just a bit.

Kim sighed and strode forward to drop an overnight bag on top of the orderly rank of suitcases. She stood just behind me. My back ached to feel her palm against it.

"It makes sense this way, hon. I feel relieved, better than I have in a long time. I bet if you examined your feelings, you'd find you feel the same way."

Anger bubbled inside as I bowed my head. "I don't have a Carla to curl up with, or an Amy to whisper to me that I've done the right thing."

I closed my eyes, regretting the scathing words as soon as they left my mouth. I sensed Kim stiffen, the words obviously finding their mark. "That's okay. You'll have your career and karate classes to keep you company," she replied in a quiet, scornful tone.

I reached up and tugged at my mop of short hair with all ten fingers. "Ah, hell, Kimmy. Nobody can make me as angry as you."

She smiled with enigmatic calm. "I guess that's my special charm."

I eyed her sideways, finding myself wanting to smile in spite of the pain and rage I was feeling. "Do you still care for me?" I asked, wheedling like a child.

Kim lifted her eyes to the ceiling as if seeking divine guidance. "You're the one who kicked me out, Marya. I might stay if you asked me."

"But you won't give up the others."

"I told you I would. I work with Carla, though. That would be tough, shutting her out." Her gaze was sad. And she wasn't about to give up her hard-won job in interior design. I knew that from a previous argument. Futility swamped me and I could only stand and study the woman I loved. Silence fell between us.

Three years of my life gone. Kim was walking away with them as easily as she was carrying away her well-stuffed bags. I would never be able to think fondly about our years together. The pain would destroy me. A list of if onlys rattled through my brain. If only I hadn't worked so much. If only I hadn't spent quite *so much time studying the martial art. If only I had been a more attentive lover. Then anger returned. If only Kim had remained faithful. A hard knot closed off my throat and tears threatened to blur my vision.*

"Hey, help me carry these last ones out, will you?" Kim asked hesitantly. She sighed and I knew she felt the same futility I felt. There seemed to be no easy way. It was a lose-lose situation.

I opened the front door and hefted the two largest bags. Kim gathered the rest and followed. Her Honda Accord sedan rested next to my Isuzu Trooper for the last time. I opened the door of the Honda and placed the bags onto the backseat next to some stacked boxes, holding the door wide so she could place the other bags inside. Trying to feel useful, I pressed the lock button and closed the door securely.

I stood helplessly. I couldn't find a place to put my hands, hands which seemed as if they belonged on Kim. Then Kim was in my arms, her cheek pressed against my shoulder. She was so right there, so familiar. She lifted her face and our kiss was soft and forlorn, filled with an idealized longing for what might have been. Afterward, she moved away and I felt a coldness enter the space where she'd stood.

Kim leaned against the car and stared up at the large brick home we had lived in for the past three years. She rubbed her thinly clad arms, shivering in the early evening chill.

"I'm sorry we can't love one another anymore," I whispered finally.

"That's not it. We're just traveling in different directions. It happens."

We fell silent, mulling over this obvious truth. A cool mist began to fall and Kim shivered again.

"Marya, if you ever need anything..." Her voice cracked in mid-sentence.

I nodded and, unable to speak because that damned lump was choking me again, I grimaced in what I hoped was a smile and waved Kim away. I turned and walked into the house. Closing the door, I heard the engine of Kim's car purr into life, a perfect counterpoint to the silent and dying memories filling the rooms behind me. I pressed my face to the heavy wooden door panel.

"But I need you," I whispered.

Marya woke in a cold sweat, an anguished cry of need reverberating in her mind. She remembered how she had loved Kim and how good it had been in the beginning. She also realized that what Kim had said was true. She *had* turned away, had turned to the martial art. Now, in the early dawn hours, in her parents' guestroom, she admitted that to herself and wondered—When had she lost interest in Kim? Why had she turned from her? What would it have taken to keep her attention steady? Would she never find someone who would hold her interest for the long haul?

CHAPTER SEVEN

The *Schuyler Times* building was located in the middle of the downtown area, just off the main street on a quiet, tree-dappled side street named Collier Lane. It appeared much the same as every other newspaper office Marya had worked in—dark and small, messy, and smelling of old ink and paper. A pleasant-looking woman sat at the desk just inside the door. She glanced up in inquiry as Marya let the door slide shut behind her.

"I'd like to apply for the reporter position you have open," Marya said, trying to smile confidently.

"Oh," the receptionist replied and then paused as if in thought. "That must be Andy's beat." She rose slowly—she was going to have a baby, Marya realized, and soon. She was obviously in the last stages of pregnancy.

"Oh no!" Marya blurted without thinking, then blushed. "I'm sorry. Here, may I help you?"

The receptionist smiled in real amusement this time, her small slanted eyes crinkling at the corners and her wide mouth showing almost as much pink gum line as teeth. "No, I've got it, but that's the exact same thing I said eight months ago when Doc Bradley told me I was in this condition: 'Oh no!'"

She laughed as she waddled away. Within minutes she was back, this time following slowly behind a rapidly moving man. He was slightly shorter than Marya's five foot eight and leaning toward portliness, with scant, dark hair combed across his ruddy scalp in a last-ditch effort to deny his baldness. His dour round face was cheered by a pair of twinkling brown eyes, jaundiced at the corners from a hard life of too many cigarettes, too much coffee and too many long hours reading copy. She knew the look well.

"Well, you must be Dick and Patty's girl. I'm Ed Bush, editor here. Tell me your name again." He eyed her sharply as he shook her hand, obviously expecting a quick response.

"Marya, Marya Brock, from Seattle," she responded hurriedly.

"Seattle, huh? You know Buzz Wheaton from out there? Runs the *Seattle Star*. Good man, Buzz."

Marya smiled with delight. This was common ground. "Yes, sir, I worked for Mister Wheaton for ten years."

The editor let fly a low whistle. "Brock? You're not that guy Brocklyn, are you? The way Buzz talked about you I always pictured you as a man."

She smiled, fondly remembering her old boss. It had been hard to leave him. "I'm not surprised, sir. He never called me anything but Brocklyn, and I'm sure that's how he referred to me when talking to others." She almost turned in response as she imagined she heard his bellow of "Brocklyn, get in here now," echoing around this newsroom.

Ed Bush studied her from head to toe. "Well, you're no guy, but with your reputation, his loss is my gain and as soon as I get the chance I'm going to call him and give him hell for not setting you up with me. Didn't he know where you were moving to?"

"Yes, he did. He gave me a letter of recommendation, but I'm sure it's generic. I mean, I could have applied at any paper in this area."

Ed grinned suddenly. "Come with me. I've got to see this letter."

He led the way through the small newsroom and down a long hallway. Feeling curious glances thrown her way from the other employees, Marya chanced a few small smiles at them and got a few back in return. The people here seemed friendly enough, she decided.

The editor led her into his small, cluttered office, which reeked of cigarette smoke. Stacks of inky newspapers framed his large, old-fashioned wooden desk, and bookshelves chock full of outdated books and periodicals spanned the wall behind his chair. Taking this chair firmly in hand, he spun it around and plopped himself into it, causing a welter of metal shrieks to fill the still air. He motioned her toward the other chair.

"Okay, let's see the letter."

She pulled the envelope from her briefcase and handed it across the desk. He took it and again motioned for her to sit.

She turned, closing her briefcase, and saw that the only other chair was occupied by a very large cat. Tabby gray in color, the cat, an old tom by the look of him, was clearly well loved and well fed. He purred contentedly and arched his neck as if seeking a stroke from her hand. Chuckling at his silent demand, she set the briefcase aside and lifted him from the chair into her arms, sliding her bottom into the warm spot he'd vacated. She buried her nose in his scentless fur and felt his sides heave as he purred with each breath.

She felt very good here, very much at home. She hoped that she would get the job.

The rustle of paper distracted her; Ed had shoved something across the desk. A tan envelope had been inside the larger white one. She had to laugh at the writing on the outside. There, in Mr. Wheaton's distinctive scrawl were the words: *Ed Bush, The Schuyler Times, You old goat.*

"Has he got me pegged or what?" the editor said with a laugh as he perused the note that had been inside. "It says here I'm to treat you right because you'll be one hell of an asset to the *Times*. Is that true?" He turned his tired eyes on Marya.

"I can only promise my best effort, Mr. Bush." Marya met his gaze evenly.

He stood abruptly and handed her the white envelope.

"There's another letter in there in case you ever need it, one of the generic kind. Buzz and I go back a long way, you know. We went through about ten years of school together, beginning in elementary school and ending up at the same college. Odd we ended up on opposite ends of the country."

He came from behind his desk and moved to the door.

"It's deadline day on the B-front. Get to work."

"You mean I've got the job?" She stood and tried not to stare at him.

Ed glanced back while lighting a fresh cigarette.

"Of course, if you want it. I'll get Carol to settle you in, but you've got to set Caesar down. We call him the energy drain. Every time you hold him for any length of time he just sort of sucks all the get-up-and-go right out of you."

Marya replaced the cat gently into the chair with one final pat.

"Not a good idea on deadline day," she muttered to the editor's retreating back. She grabbed her briefcase and hurried to catch up, ready to go to work.

CHAPTER EIGHT

The outside walls of The Way of Hand and Foot gleamed in the rising sunlight as Dorry pulled into the parking area and slotted her truck into the reserved spot next to the side entrance.

She sat back and sighed, her gaze falling fondly on the lacy crepe myrtle trees she had planted next to the building soon after purchasing the low, flat structure. The trio of trees had just finished blooming and a few remaining bedraggled pink flowers winked at her as they danced in an early morning breeze.

Over to her left, by the front door, she had commissioned a beautiful waterfall that fell smoothly into a shallow, concave rock and water garden. Late water lilies nodded there as if reluctant to awaken this early. She opened the truck door so she could hear the soft susurrus of water falling into water. It was a beautiful South Carolina morning.

She keenly recalled her fear when she'd actually realized she was buying a building and creating a business. That she was sinking her family's hard-earned money into a venture that could win or fail by the vagaries of people, the economy and of willful, destructive nature. She took in a deep breath, reminding herself that had been many years ago now and that the *dojang* was thriving.

In spite of her reputation.

Lifting her cell phone from the bench seat, she pressed a button and saw that three more calls had come in during her short drive to the *dojang*. And this all before seven a.m. She sighed again, wondering how best to handle the situation. She really had no desire to talk to her, feeling like they had already said everything that needed to be said. Yet she had sounded frazzled, like something was wrong.

Frowning and steeling her resolve, Dorry snatched her duffel off the seat and left the truck, cell phone in hand. She unlocked the thick steel door and entered the back hallway of the *dojang*. Back here she could smell the cleaning fluid used by Ella Mae who cleaned for her three nights a week. Progressing along the hallway, pausing only to toss the duffel full of her street clothes on the couch in her office, she was soon inundated with the welcome smells of rubber mats, steel and sweat from the *dojang*.

She pulled her belt from the pocket of her *dobok* and fingered its worn, shredded edges. She'd had this belt a long time. Many years. She remembered her first belt, a yellow one as was standard for the discipline she had always followed. She'd been fourteen at the time, a young girl reeling from the death of her mother. In the martial art she'd found solace and a sense of family, a sense of accomplishment. Feelings that losing a mother to cancer had stripped from her.

Then when Francie had died…when everything had been lost to her…she'd come back to the art with renewed vigor, finding solace in the familiar.

And now there were the phone calls that were renewing those feelings of loss, feelings best ignored. What did Izzie want from her?

Without thinking about it, her movements practiced and economical, Dorry wrapped the soft belt three times about her waist and then settled it into a familiar knot at the front of her uniform. She slid from her sandals and stood facing the Korean and American flags that adorned the wall at the front of the *dojang*. She bowed and spoke the motto of her *dojang* as a sort of ritual prayer:

"Courage first. Power second. Technique third."

How she loved this room and this building. Deciding to stay in Schuyler Point had been tough, but it was her home; everything dear and familiar was here. Once her mind was made up to stay, she had simply dug in her heels and focused on making The Way of Hand and Foot a success. She'd kept prices low and pretty much lived at the *dojang* to ensure that success. And it had worked, a sure sign from the universe that she had been meant to stay in the town she'd been born and bred in.

Dorry strolled over to a long black bag mounted vertically in a back corner of the room. Suspended from the ceiling by a strong rope anchored to the concrete floor, this bag had seen many years of abuse. Heavy silver tape was wrapped around it for strength, and even frayed by wear, its massive bulk easily overpowered that corner of the room.

Dorry removed shoe and hand pads from a nearby cabinet after laying her cell phone on top of it. Donning the gear, she tried to clear her mind of everything. She tried. Oddly enough, her thoughts kept straying to the altercation on Dundun Beach. Kept lingering on her remembered image of the woman. Remembering the powerful arms that had held her close.

Dorry scowled, angry that her thoughts had betrayed her when she needed surcease. If she wasn't thinking about

Izzie, she was thinking about this one, this redhead. All Dorry wanted was to be left alone. She'd been alone for years now and that was just the way she liked it. She glanced at the wall behind the bag and read the bright placard she'd placed there when outfitting the *dojang*. It was her favorite quote, from Aristotle.

We are what we repeatedly do.
Excellence, then, is not an act, but a habit.

She nodded in silent agreement. She'd become good at being alone. She'd be damned if she'd let anyone change that.

Still, she checked her phone one more time. No new calls. Perversely disappointed, she slammed the phone back onto the cabinet, then attacked the body bag with a deep anger bordering on lunacy. Dust enveloping her as it flew from the bag into the still morning air, she kicked and punched until she was exhausted, her muscles quivering from exertion. She put one palm on the bag, steadying it as she gasped for air. She eyed the phone and scowled before beginning a second round of attack.

CHAPTER NINE

I don't know why they didn't want me. Mama always said it was because they loved their career best and I would have come in a distant second. A distant second. As if I was even in the running.

I stared out across Sawyer Lake, my mind rehashing Mama's anger last night. She'd been drinking again and I really hated that. She got mean when she drank bourbon...or anything else, for that matter. Any alcohol. She would go on and on about how everyone had betrayed her and how I always had to be hidden from sight. That we had to be so careful. That we could never be seen together.

If people found out about me then the woman would never pay more money. As if she ever would anyway. I think she figured out of sight, out of mind. Maybe it would be best to tell everyone about it. Get it all out in the open.

I wondered sometimes if Mama was just making excuses because she didn't like the way I looked. Or how I acted.

I sighed and shifted my position. Sawyer Lake was one of the few freshwater lakes in Schuyler Point, and Mama and me used to come here once in a while when I was little. But only during times when no one else was there. Today the little lake beach was peppered with fat little families, mommies, daddies and pudgy, whiny-faced children. I hated all of them.

Last Tuesday the beach had been deserted and I had been bad. Bad like Mama didn't want me to be bad. I had been over to Lucy's house. She had given me vodka and then painted my face like hers so that my eyes were black all around and my eyelashes thick and heavy with mascara. She left for work but since I had that day off, I'd come out here.

No one knew about it, but that day I had put three of my little glass bottles in the trunk.

I loved my little bottles. They were just beer bottles that I kept down in the basement. Every now and then I would go down there, usually when Mama was at work, and I would carefully fill them with lots of saltpeter and fertilizer, bought at Anderson's Hardware, and then top them off with kerosene from the heater tank. Sometimes, depending on where the bottles would go, I would add some pebbles or pieces of broken glass. Usually I fixed the fuses in with white paraffin, but I had used red candle wax on these because we were out of paraffin.

The ones I had used Tuesday held broken glass. I had just wanted to kill fish, that was all, and I had, a ton of them, but when the little Koffman girl had run up on the beach, bleeding, earlier today…well, that was just gravy.

CHAPTER TEN

Marya settled in quickly at the *Schuyler Times*. She pitched in as a runner that first hectic day, doing whatever hack job was necessary to get the second section of the paper together. The next day was pretty much the same as everyone worked to finish off the front section, and Carol Say, the pregnant receptionist, introduced her to her new co-workers.

The staff was larger than she had expected, two staff writers besides herself and about a half dozen or so additional employees.

Marvin Torn, who covered the political beat, wore a tie and a three-piece suit to work and was meticulously groomed. Dallas Myerson, a tiny slip of a lady, very proper, handled the social and activities beat. Marya was going to be the paper's feature reporter, an assignment which pleased her greatly. She enjoyed writing about people and their lives and abhorred the endless council meetings that a regular top-half-of-the-front-page news reporter such as Marvin had to cover.

Carol, the receptionist, was consistently sweet and made her feel very much at home that first day. Carol was married to Buddy and he was there at noon bringing lunch and hovering.

Other staff members included copy editor Denton Hyde, a distinguished older gentleman who dressed in immaculately pressed trousers and Oxford shirts. He was unusually quiet, perhaps shy, but seemed to know the newspaper business inside and out. She came to admire him and his quiet advice within the space of just a few hours.

Plump, gray-haired Emily Davies was the business manager for the newspaper. She controlled the advertising accounts with an iron hand, but otherwise was an earth mother to everyone. Carol told Marya that Emily brought in at least two homemade cakes or pies a week, urging all of them to eat.

The production crew, responsible for putting the printed stories on the newsprint page in coherent fashion, was made up of two rowdy, jolly, joking men whose working styles seemed to mesh like clockwork. Wallace and Craig, whose last names she didn't catch in the din of the pressroom, liked to tease the girls of the office, tossing bawdy remarks back and forth across the layout tables as they flashed scissors and X-Acto knives with alarming speed and intensity.

Three other employees, who were mysteriously in and out at any time, were Connie Doalin, who worked in advertising and circulation, Skip Pleasants, who wrote the sports page on a part-time basis, and Kenny Bond, the paper's sole photographer.

The *Schuyler Times* was a small weekly of about twenty-four pages total, so, although the pace was hectic, the work was over quickly and the photographic plates of each page safely off to the press in Myrtle Beach by eight o'clock Tuesday evening.

Marya was sitting with Marvin, Dallas and Emily, enjoying a cup of the heavy office coffee and the glow of having helped put another paper to bed, when a familiar name was mentioned.

"Hey, Marya, has Ed given you the Dorcas Wood assignment yet?" Marvin grinned at her like a schoolboy.

She shook her head in the negative. "No, what assignment?"

"I don't know why y'all can't leave Dorry alone," Denton said in his soft voice. He sat to one side, perusing the Richmond, Virginia, paper.

"Well, she's just bein' silly, is all," piped Dallas in her lilting drawl. "There's no sense in a body bein' so selfish."

Marya's curiosity was piqued. "Selfish? Selfish, how?"

Dallas laughed and winked at Emily. "I guess you're just goin' to have to find that out for yourself now, aren't you, hon? That's part of the job. All the new reporters have to interview ol' Dorry. Why, she's just a legend in these parts. Isn't that so, Marvin?"

"Sure is," Marvin agreed, adding, "all you have to do is go to that karate place of hers and ask her for an interview. We want a regular lifestyle feature. You know, what made her get involved in karate and stick with it. Most women give it up quick, just can't make the grade against the guys, but she's been at it for more than twenty years. That's pretty impressive if you ask me."

Marya bristled at his mocking tone but kept her composure. Having earned five belts in taekwondo, she knew precisely how hard it was. She also knew that all women didn't simply give it up when confronted by harsh conditions. That was not what the sport was all about.

"That's it? That's the assignment? How hard can it be?" She looked expectantly from face to face.

Dallas and Marvin exchanged amused glances.

Denton rustled his newspaper and folded it neatly. "Don't let them tease you, Miss Brock. Dorry's had a lot of...well, let's say notoriety, in her life and has no love of reporters. The media have not been kind to her. I am positive she will not talk to you."

Marya sighed and stood, smoothing her trousers. "Well, nothing ventured, nothing gained. Actually, I had planned to stop by her studio anyway to check on something else, so I'll take the assignment."

"Good luck!" Marvin called after her. She heard Emily laughing as the door to the newsroom swung closed behind her.

To her delight, she found Dorcas Wood's *dojang* easily. It was located south of town on Rosemont, Schuyler Point's main street, just before it turned into the main highway leading to North Myrtle Beach. It was a low, wide, severe building, but someone had obviously done a lot of work on the structure. It was landscaped and freshly painted and a large central sign bore the English translation of taekwondo as the name of the *dojang*, The Way of Hand and Foot.

She parked her car in the crowded parking lot and, fetching up her slender reporter's notebook, strode confidently toward the door, expecting to impress this Dorcas Wood completely. As soon as she entered however, her righteous conviction began to evaporate, blown away by so much mystic wind.

The front lobby was wide but not deep. A desk, uncluttered and simple, stood to the left. Mounted on the wall in front of her, on either side of the two black-enameled doors leading into the *dojang* proper, were ten framed pictures. Their familiarity tugged at her, and she was drawn over to them as if riding on well-oiled wheels. The pictures, painted in the Chinese calligraphy style, with a brush and black ink, stretched along that entire wall, five on each side of the door, each in a matching shiny black frame.

She knew these, as did every martial artist worth his salt. These were the legendary ox-herding pictures, graphic representations of the Zen master's search for Buddhahood.

The first image showed a tree-bordered field of grass. To one side swept a graceful willow tree; a sparkling river, bounded by large boulders, raced through the picture behind it. Off to the far right side, almost unnoticed, stood a small girl child, one tiny hand lifted to her mouth in indecision.

The second painting was almost identical to the first except now the girl child held a length of rope in her small hands and was following an ox that was partially visible in the trees.

In the next one, the girl was attempting to pass the rope around the neck of the wild beast, but it was a struggle, as the ox appeared to be pulling away.

As the story unfolded in the next paintings, the child captured the wild ox and tamed it, eventually playing music on a flute with the docile creature at her feet.

Marya strode slowly along the rank of paintings, her eyes glued to the various nuances of meaning until she reached the final one, a large circle, empty but full of the no thing, the one thing that martial artists seek. She knew then that this school was the one true school that she had been looking for since starting her training so many years ago. From the absence of trophies in the lobby, she knew that competition and winning tournaments was not what this school was about. Instead, the paintings, representing man's battle with his undisciplined self, let her know that the taekwondo students at this *dojang* were on a spiritual quest as well as a physical one. Sudden happiness washed through her.

"Hello. May I help you?" The strong voice came from her left and she saw that a uniformed woman had entered the lobby from a side door and was bent at the desk writing something in a large notebook.

"Yes, thank you. I'm looking for Dorcas Wood." Marya approached the desk.

The woman raised up to look at her with cautious slowness. She lifted eyes of a clear cornflower blue. They were familiar eyes. Marya realized that she was the woman from the beach, the one who had rescued her that first night in town. These eyes were serene but wary as they studied her, recognized her.

Marya studied her right back and realized again what a striking woman she was. And how muscular. She dominated the lobby completely. There was a type of energy emanating from her, a kind of low hum that Marya sensed more than heard.

Unnerved by the energy as well as the calm gaze, Marya tried to focus on the woman's appearance and found it very hard to do. She noticed that the short cap of hair was snow white, with just a wisp of darker color around the temples. Her skin bore healthy color, the ruddy tan of much time spent outdoors, and this contrast was further enhanced by those piercing blue eyes.

The woman was dressed in a master's uniform, black trousers and tunic, speckled with various patches of achievement and rank. Marya knew then that she was looking at Dorcas Wood.

"Miss Wood," she stammered, her throat inexplicably dry. "My name is Marya Brock. I'd like to study with you."

Master Wood's gaze wavered a bit but remained cautious. "Have you studied before?"

"Yes, four years under Master Hayes in Seattle, Washington."

Master Wood nodded. Oddly enough, she seemed to be studying Marya's shoes.

"Rank?"

"First black."

She turned to the desk and opened a drawer. "Which means *Kebong*? *Il jang*? *E jang*? *Sam jong*? *Sim jong*?"

"Yes, ma'am." Marya sighed, glad the forms and stylized dances of this school were the same as her old school. "All of those and currently *O jong*. Also the fighting forms, *sabong chucks*."

She nodded, her mouth twitching in what Marya took to mean approval, and pulled a form from the drawer. "Anything else?"

"I'm trained in *hapkido*."

Master Wood turned her full attention on Marya, her eyes cutting through her like a knife. "Ah, the grappling art."

She paused a long beat. "Tell me. How does it make you feel to know that you can disable a person in seconds with this skill?"

Marya chafed under the question, remembering all the hard work it took to learn the subtleties of movement *hapkido* required. Yes, it was a very dangerous art, but she owed the master no apologies. "I feel grateful I can protect myself should the need arise," she said finally.

Master Wood was watching her again and silence stretched taut between them. Marya waited her out. Eventually, the master handed her the form. "Everything you need to know about fees and rules is here. Please fill out the bottom part and bring it with you when you come to class."

Marya took the form.

"Now, tell me why you are really here," she said abruptly.

Marya quaked inside, then realized the master must have seen the notebook clutched in her hand. "I...I'm to interview you."

"Interview me?" Her smile was brittle, her voice sarcastic.

"Yes, for the newspaper, *The Schuyler Times*. About your life..."

"My life..." She shook her head from side to side with eyes closed, then looked at Marya. "What do you know about my life?"

"Nothing. That's why..." She shrugged, feeling suddenly helpless.

"So you thought you'd trot on down here and open up old Dorry like a can of peaches. Then invite the whole county in to have a look inside, see what makes Dorry tick.

Is that right?" Master Wood waited for an answer, her glare belligerent.

Anger swelled inside Marya. "Now, look here. I was just given the assignment..."

"No, miss, you look here." Fury darkened the master's gaze and abrupt fear surrounded Marya's own anger. "I'm sorely tired of you reporters sniffing around after me like dogs after a bitch in heat. People who know me know I like to be left alone. It's just you new, pasty-faced, snot-nosed little reporters who are stupid enough to take the bait—to come down here and pull my chain. Now, don't you feel stupid? I'm sure old Ed Bush is down there just laughing his fool head off at you."

Her sarcastic tone bludgeoned Marya, knocking off pieces of confidence as surely as any real weapon. Marya's face flushed and equal parts of anger and hurt raged within her. Then that Irish temper took over and once again words spewed from her before she could think about them.

"What is your problem, anyway? Is your life so precious that you have to keep it under lock and key? I don't deserve this kind of crap from you. I'm just trying to do my job. Some of us don't have fancy businesses of our own and actually have to do what others tell them to, you know."

She took a deep breath and raged on. "Besides, if I were a hard-core investigative reporter, you'd be shaking in your shoes right about now 'cause I wouldn't give up. I'd be like a hyena tracking a gazelle going after your butt, until I learned everything there was to learn about you with or without your help. How would you like that? Huh? Are there any skeletons in your closet, Miss Wood?"

Marya angrily flipped open the lid of her notebook and poised her pen above the page. "You want to talk now? No? You'd rather I did the work for you? I've been wanting to do a little investigative journalism anyway."

They glared at one another as Marya tried to get her breathing under control. As Marya watched Master Wood, her eyes and face feeling hard as flint, she saw Master Wood's gaze change. It softened in a subtle way; maybe there was sadness there. But if it was sadness, there was a steel edge to it, as her gaze remained locked with Marya's. Abruptly, without changing her demeanor in the slightest, she turned and strode through the side door, leaving Marya standing alone in the lobby.

CHAPTER ELEVEN

Mama found the Silvestres' cat right off. I should have known.

She was standing on the porch when I drove up, her white dress blinding bright in the high beams of my headlights. The dead cat, mauled and partially skinned, dangled from one hand.

I closed the car door quietly and approached her. I tilted my head down, hoping she could sense how sorry I was. Only I knew it was not for the cat, of course, but because she'd found it.

"Well," she began, eying me harshly in the twilight dimness. "What do you have to say for yourself?"

I scrubbed my palms along the front of my T-shirt, in my imagination again feeling the cat's warm blood there on my stomach.

"It pestered me, Mama. Every night when the windows were open it would come crawl in bed with me, bringing its fleas and God-all knows what else. The other night I just couldn't do it anymore." I hung my head again.

"And it's just too damn hot to shut the window, is that it?" she asked, swinging the cat slowly to and fro.

I was hopeful for a brief moment but realized she was just setting me up. No way was I going to get away with this one.

"No, Mama, I shoulda shut it."

Silence fell between us for a long beat. I glanced up to see a deeply thoughtful look on her face.

"What're you thinking, Mama?" I asked, keeping my voice low and soft.

She was suddenly all business. "Don't you worry none about that, child." She held the cat toward me.

"You need to do something about this, though, and don't put it back in the root cellar. Don't you know it'll start stinkin' to high heaven, you leave it there? Use some sense, now, pay attention."

"Yes, Mama," I replied, taking the cat from her. I waited for the slap that never came and a small smile nibbled its way across my lips. I carried the cat away, off toward the woods.

CHAPTER TWELVE

Dorry had had just about enough. The constant calls and messages were too much. Izzie never said much in the messages she left in her voice mail box, just a simple "Call me, please. It's important." That somehow made it worse. If it had been something easy or even a heartfelt "I miss you, Dorry," it would have been okay. This, this had to be something else.

Dorry rose and closed the door to her office, effectively shutting out the slams and chi calls of her belts and students. She was calling from her office because she knew there was a chance she would be interrupted and she wanted that fail-safe so the call would be a short one.

As she waited for Izzie to pick up, Dorry hated the fact that her heart was racing and that her mind had immediately gone back to what they'd once had. Once.

And then Isabel was on the line.

"It's me," Dorry said quietly.

"Oh, my gosh, I am so glad you finally returned my call," Isabel said, her words clipped and fast, subtly accented by a French pace.

"You called enough. What did you need?" Dorry asked belligerently. She didn't want to let Izzie know how much hearing her voice still affected her.

"I can't talk now. The mah jong girls are here. I wanted to let you know that I'll be coming in next week and we need to meet."

Dorry sighed. "About what, Izzie? You know coming here is not a good idea. And we definitely shouldn't be seen together."

"I know," she said in a hurried whisper. Dorry could hear women laughing in the background. "But this is important. There's been a threat."

Dorry sat straighter in her chair. "Toward me? Is it...him?"

"Yes...I'm not sure. I'll call you when I get into South Carolina."

"Okay. Okay. I'll talk to you then."

"Dorry?"

"Yes?"

"Please be careful. I do still love you, you know."

Dorry closed her eyes and her voice was a whisper when she replied. "I know."

The line went dead, and Dorry suffered a conflict of emotions. A part of her wanted to be elated by Isabel's last words, yet she knew that way led to madness. Their love simply could not be. Would never be again.

She severed the phone connection on her end and placed her phone on the desk.

A threat. That's all she needed. Things had gotten bad after Little Bit died, but that had been years ago. Her stalker had finally faded away when she pressed charges. Now, it appeared that all of it was coming back to bite her on the ass in one way or another. Add to that the nosy reporter who'd been sniffing around and Dorry had way more than she wanted to deal with.

Her thoughts drifted to the reporter. She had been brave that afternoon on the beach. Dorry had seen her square off, go into horse stance, as she had been trained, ready for battle. That was impressive. Seeing her close up afterward had given Dorry pause. She seemed so young, but her eyes had been wise and that hug...well, Dorry had yet to forget that hug.

What about her threats today? Would she really dredge up all that old dirt? Dorry shuddered. Wouldn't that just be peachy? There was nothing she could do about it now; things were in motion that she had no control over. Wearily, she rose and moved toward the door. Things would unfold as they would.

She paused after opening the door as a new thought occurred to her. She would see Isabel next week. She didn't know whether to be thrilled or terrified.

CHAPTER THIRTEEN

Denton had taken the day off to have his yearly physical, and Marya was proofing the classifieds for him. The simple, straightforward advertisement caught her eye immediately. "Cottage for rent," it read and then listed the number of a local realty firm. She reached for the telephone.

"Coastal Realty," said a piping female voice on the second ring.

"I'm interested in the advertisement in the *Schuyler Times*. About the cottage for rent," Marya said.

"Oh, that's probably Henry Giles's listing. I'll get him for you if you don't mind holding."

She told the receptionist that she didn't mind and was treated to an immediate flood of lilting, low-decibel music. She hummed along with Barry Manilow for half a song before he was switched off abruptly.

"Henry Giles," stated a young, but self-assured male voice. "How can I help you?"

Marya told him her name and asked about the cottage.

"Oh yes, that's a nice place. Kind of small, though. Do you have children?"

"No, I plan to live alone," she answered.

"Then it will be perfect, I'm sure. I just thought, in all fairness, I'd let you know that up front."

"Oh, I appreciate that. So tell me more about the cottage."

"Let's see."

She heard the distant rustle of paper.

"It's one bedroom, living room, a large kitchen and a fully furnished bath. It's got this big wraparound porch and its location is prime, right on the water of Begaman Cove."

"And the price?" She tried to hide her mounting excitement. After all, you can't tell much about a place until you see it and hear how much it'll cost.

"Low, if you ask me. Just four hundred fifty a month for the entire cottage and use of all the land adjacent to it," he said with a sigh.

"When can I see it?"

Again the rustle of paper.

"How's three thirty today sound? I'm free then."

She agreed with enthusiasm and wrote down detailed directions, thrilled by the possibility of a new home at last. True, she wouldn't own it, but she was strangely at ease with that idea. If truth be told, she thought she enjoyed her footloose status. Everything she did had an experimental flavor and she was beginning to enjoy the feeling of starting her life anew with different parameters than before.

***

The cottage looked to be more than adequate. Situated about five hundred feet from the serene water of Begaman Cove and framed by a copse of scrub pines and cedar brush, the small wood bungalow glimmered, the glass of many large windows reflecting the early afternoon sunlight. Weathered wooden shingles covered the slanted roof, and the outer walls were constructed of large planks nailed together in an intricate pattern of descending angles. The extensive deck, just as modern as the rest of the structure, had been stained a dark mahogany, which added to the overall nouveau-rustic appearance. Marya decided it was very attractive.

She moved away from her car and walked toward the front door, which faced half-round to the cove. The ocean wind was stronger on this side, and empty planters, which were hanging from the edges of the wooden awning, swayed hypnotically. The well-built deck was sturdy under her feet. To her surprise, the brass knob in the wood and glass front door turned. The house was unlocked. Holding onto the knob with one hand, she knocked with the other and she stepped inside.

"Mr. Giles?" she called. "It's Marya Brock, here about the cottage."

There was no response, but she entered the large pleasant front room anyway, hoping the owner and the realtor were not the sorts who press charges for unlawful entry. The inside was completely, but simply, furnished, another plus. An adorable potbelly wood-burning stove occupied a place of honor in the center of the large living area. The bedroom, right off the main room, featured little more than a double bed, two end tables, a small closet and one tall bureau. Still, that was more than enough to meet her needs. The bath was small, but pleasant, the shower wide and bordered by a wall of glass bricks. The sparkling clean kitchen, part of the open living area, was large and airy, with many tall windows looking directly onto the cove. She stood for a moment and watched gulls vying for one another's attention as they frolicked in the air above the small curved beach. The water, fading from greenish blue near the beach to the blue of midnight farther out, moved with sluggish restlessness as it ignored the drama unfolding among the gulls just above it. Far out on the ocean horizon, she saw a hazy body of land. Unable, after many moments, to figure out exactly where the land lay, she pulled her eyes away.

A figure snared Marya's attention as it strode from a forested copse onto the reddish sand of the beach. She watched as the figure moved closer and realized that this person was coming straight toward the cottage. Perhaps it was the owner. She walked rapidly through the house and out the front door, not stopping until she reached the front bumper of the Trooper. It wouldn't do for the owner to find her browsing through his house unattended.

Waiting, she began counting to herself to dispel a sudden nervousness. One would think after more than a decade of reporting on people's lives, she would feel at ease with strangers. Not so. She often clenched up when it came time to meet someone new. After what seemed an interminable time, the owner rounded the corner of the house. It was Dorcas Wood. Marya's nervousness leapt up and increased tenfold.

When Dorry saw Marya she stopped and impaled her with those keen, bright blue eyes. Marya watched her as well, maintaining as steady a regard as possible. After almost a full minute, she was puzzled to see a wave of resignation flicker across the woman's eagle gaze.

"So, it's you," she said. "I should have known. Guess I pegged you wrong after all. You're going to be one of the ones who just won't give up. I suppose I should have paid more attention to your fancy threats."

It took Marya a moment to realize what she was talking about. When she did, she became angry. "This has nothing to do with the story. I need a place to live," she retorted, trying to keep her tone calm.

Dorry resumed walking and continued around to the front of the cottage. "Well, you're not living here."

Marya's mouth dropped open at the abrupt dismissal, and she strode after her. "What do you mean, I can't live here? Are you afraid I won't be able to pay the rent?"

Dorry paused before entering the cottage, one hand poised on the edge of the open door, and regarded her with steely calm. "I'll not have you spying on me. I'm sorry. You'll just have to find another place."

"Find another place! But I like it here," Marya cried as she stepped onto the deck. She tried the front door; anger flared as she realized Dorry had locked it after entering the house. She was tempted to kick in the door, but she tried to maintain her composure. Dorry'd never rent to her if she proved destructive.

"Look, Miss Wood," she called through the door, cupping her hands around her face and leaning close to peer through the glass. "I really like this cottage. I'm living with my parents and I need to move out. Please reconsider."

Marya could see her through the window of the door. She was sitting at the kitchen table, her square hands wiping at the tabletop with a paper towel. She was pointedly ignoring Marya.

Marya slammed the edge of one fist against the wooden doorjamb, unable to help herself. The sound echoed throughout the cove, giving her a certain satisfaction. She wished it had landed on Dorcas Wood's stubborn head instead.

Marya stomped across the deck and walked with heavy tread around to the driveway. Just as she was getting into her Trooper, a small blue car pulled alongside.

"I'm so sorry I'm late, Miss Brock. Someone bought a house at the last minute and I got bogged down in paperwork. I called the owner, Dorry Wood. Did she show you around?"

Henry Giles was much as she had pictured him—young, handsome, athletic in build. Now, as he apologized, he brushed absently at his thinning blond hair and watched her expectantly.

"She showed me around all right," she told him, her tone sullen. "She showed me the way out. She won't rent to me."

He seemed perplexed. "But why? Did she tell you why?"

She shrugged her shoulders. "I'm not sure. I believe it's because she thinks I'll spy on her or something."

"Spy on her?" Giles laughed, then sobered. "Well, legally she's got to give you the reason on paper. Let's go see what's on her mind."

He led the way around the house. She followed doubtfully. She figured once Dorcas Wood's mind was made up, it stayed that way.

Pulling a tagged key from his pocket, Giles soon had them inside.

"Now, Henry, don't come annoying me about this girl. I'm not renting to her and that's that," said Dorry as she rose from her chair at the table.

"But why, Dorry?" Giles asked quietly. "We need to talk about this."

Dorry fixed her irritating stare on Marya. "She's a reporter, Henry. That's all that needs to be said."

Giles quieted in thought and then motioned Marya outside. "Let me talk to her, Miss Brock. Why don't you step down to the beach?"

As Marya closed the door she could hear Dorry lashing into the realtor. Great sadness filled her. She guessed she wasn't meant to live there after all. Unwilling to stick around for the dismal outcome, she slid into her car and drove back to work, hoping there would be something in tomorrow's rental ads.

Back at the newspaper office, Marya found herself unable to concentrate. The story she was doing about a woman who lived with fourteen dogs just wouldn't come together. She found herself falling into a mild depression, taking out her lingering anger and frustration by snapping at a bewildered Dallas.

It rankled that Dorcas Wood hated her so absolutely. Marya had done her no real harm, at least not on purpose.

If only she had approached her differently, she thought, if she hadn't been dumb enough to act as Marvin's patsy, things could have been different between them.

It wasn't just the idea of losing the cottage. Another adequate place would come along, she was sure. There was the whole question of studying under Dorry, something Marya realized she desperately wanted. A student necessarily had to be on good terms with her instructor, especially in martial arts training, which can be hazardous if mishandled. She thought again of the framed pictures in the lobby of The Way of Hand and Foot and wanted to scream in frustration.

This insanity had to be some sort of a test, she told herself, gazing blindly at her computer screen.

"Hey, Marya," Carol called, pulling her from her self-torture. "Phone for you on line two. And it's a maaan!" She raised her eyebrows suggestively, and Marya frowned at her as she picked up the call.

"Miss Brock? This is Henry Giles."

"Oh, Mr. Giles, listen, I'm really sorry for causing so much trouble. I can't understand why she dislikes me. I've never done anything to her, I swear."

"Please, don't worry about it. Dorry is just that way. She eats reporters for breakfast. Don't let her ruffle you. Once you get to know her, you'll find she's quite reasonable. She's got a good head on her shoulders."

"That may be, but, if you don't mind, I think I'll avoid Miss Wood in the future."

He laughed. "Funny, those were her exact same words about you. That's why you'll pay your rent through my office. I hope that won't be a problem for you?"

Marya fell silent, wondering if she'd heard him correctly. "What do you mean? Did I get the cottage?"

"Sure. Did you doubt it?"

"She said she wouldn't rent to me!"

Giles chuckled. "Dorry says a lot of things. After a few minutes, I got her to see reason. Being a realtor,

I'm pretty persuasive, especially when it comes to making money. You do still want it, don't you?"

"Yes, yes, of course," Marya said, smiling so broadly that her face hurt. "How on earth did you get her to agree to it?"

"I just told her what a nice person you are, so you'd better not disappoint me on that front. I gave her my word that you would never bother her or spy on her or anything, so I hope that's not what's on your mind. If it is, you'd better tell me now."

He paused expectantly and Marya hastened to reassure him her intentions were honorable.

"Good. Any problems you have with the cottage call me, not her. All business dealings are to be through me, okay?"

"Absolutely!"

"Good. Can you drop by here this afternoon after work? I'll wait for you because there's some papers you need to sign and I need the first month's rent and a month's deposit. Then you can move in whenever you like."

"Thank you. Yes, I'll be there. In about half an hour, in fact." Marya was delirious with relief. Maybe, with time, Dorry would reconsider her feelings about her, as well.

"I'm on Preston, just off Collier. Go down two stoplights, turn right and you'll see a big sign out front, Coastal Realty."

"Yes, got it," Marya said as she scribbled the directions.

"And remember, leave Dorry be. She has a temper and I'd hate to see you on the receiving end of it. Anything you need should be handled through this office. Don't forget."

"I won't," she said, heart chilling anew despite her excitement.

CHAPTER FOURTEEN

I knew where she'd been. Watching the house again. It's what she always did when she had a day off and sometimes even during the day when she pretended to be working. I'm not sure why she hated the woman so much. They'd been friends once or so she said. Sometimes I doubted it.

I closed my phone and tapped it against my chin as I looked around to make sure no one else was nearby. The house appeared to be deserted. Mama said she had parked at a house just down the road a ways so his was the only car parked in front.

The man was following her. She told me she had led him into the woods west of the house. I left my car and started along the edge of the wooded area. Then I saw him. He was standing next to a tree, wearing a pale blue shirt and tan trousers. He was older than I expected but that was okay; maybe he would back off easier. He was watching something, one finger crooked around his chin. I figured it was Mama.

I followed his gaze and had to swallow hard. Mama stood in a clearing, her shirt off and fanning herself with a handkerchief. The white of her bra was blinding in the forest and I looked away, embarrassed.

I moved closer to the man and grabbed him from behind, pinning his arms to his sides. He cried out and Mama was there within seconds.

"What are you doing, spying on my mama," I whispered against his ear. He craned his neck to look back at me.

"It *is* you," he said, eyes wide.

Mama was shrugging into her blouse. "There's an envelope in the front seat of his car," she said. "Get his keys."

I fished in his trouser pocket and pulled out a key ring. I handed it to her.

"What now?" I asked and the man grunted.

"Yes, what will you do now? She will find out, you know, and she will tell," he told Mama.

"And that will be a good thing," she replied, straightening her collar. "But it will be on my schedule, not yours. You had no business nosing around."

"They're both like sisters to me. I won't let you blackmail her any longer. It's just wrong."

Mama got that angry look in her eyes. "What's wrong is him not living up to his responsibilities...and them thinking they're so much better than the rest of us. That's wrong."

"Listen," he began, but Mama cut him off.

"No, you listen. My sweet baby is just as deserving as that other one."

She looked at me. "Take him over to the cellar. Tie him up tight. Then you come and pick me up at Bird Island. Hurry now, I mean it."

I recoiled. Was she asking me to…? I smiled even as my heart leapt in my chest. I could be bad. It was okay.

Mama turned away and disappeared into the trees.

"So, let's go for a little walk," I said as I goose-stepped him through the forest, heading back to the car.

CHAPTER FIFTEEN

"Brocklyn! Where the hell is Denton?" The shout came from Ed, buried in his office. This was the third time he'd asked the same question, and Marya still had no answer.

"I don't know, Ed," she called. "I haven't seen him in two days. I've told you that."

Marya sighed and returned to her perusal of plant catalogs. Settling into her new home had been going well except for her mother's determination to press her with various household staples. After the third armload of sheets and towels from her, Marya had returned it all, with the firm request her mother give her what she really needed, plants for the empty planters swaying above the cottage's deck. Bless her mother. Her feelings hadn't been hurt a bit. She had cheerfully handed Marya some catalogs and told her to write up an order for whatever she wished.

Waking each morning to the call of the gulls was becoming a pleasant addiction. Marya had taken to visiting the beach each morning before work, making note of the subtle variations of sea and sky. It seemed the ocean off Begaman Cove had developed a life of its own, choosing a new color and style for each day. The never-ending motion of the waves and the slap of foam on the shore invigorated Marya, energized her.

She found little to change in the house proper. She had merely repacked her boxes, loaded them into her car and then unpacked again. The large living area now bore most of her books and what few mementos she possessed, making the place her own. Outside, she had taken advantage of a natural rise in the yard and constructed a type of meditation garden for herself. The project had occupied and excited her for the past several days and now it was done.

Sitting at her cramped desk in the newsroom, Marya let her thoughts drift to that special place of her own and allowed a soothing peace to overtake her. She imagined herself sitting on the square wooden platform, a platform painstakingly sanded and smoothed by her own hands. She mentally inhaled the sweet smoke of incense as the small ceremonial fire warmed her face. Wind chimes sounded in a soft breeze and the rustle of bamboo fronds voiced nearby.

A sudden slam against her desk brought her back to the present with cruel harshness.

"Brock, this is getting crazy. There's no answer at his house. He hasn't called in all day. What did he do, just take off for the Bahamas? Is he having some sort of midlife crisis? Did he go gaga over some younger woman?"

Ed stared at her with helpless frustration, his palms pressing into the piles of paperwork on her desk.

"I don't know what to tell you, Ed. I haven't heard or seen anything that would help you. I wish to goodness I had." She shrugged her shoulders, eyeing him with helplessness.

"Well, move over to his desk and try to pick up some of his slack, will you? I'll get the others to help too, but stuff is piling up at his station like you wouldn't believe. When he does get back, you'd better bet he's gonna catch hell from me."

Mumbling under his breath, Ed moved toward his office.

Leaving her imaginary porch garden with some regret, Marya put away the catalogs and got back to work, moving across the way to Denton's tidy desk area. If she was going to do double duty as copyeditor and reporter, she was going to need every second of the day.

Marya didn't leave work until seven that evening when the last page of newsprint had been copy edited. She was beginning to worry about Denton. His e-mail box was overflowing; his computer was flashing with overdue messages the entire time she'd been on it. Marya didn't know him that well, but she didn't see him as the sort of irresponsible person who would take off without a word to anyone, leaving so many incomplete projects behind. He had seemed to her to be the levelheaded one in the office, the one who brought wild ideas into focus, who brought impossible story ideas back to reality. Taking a deep, needed breath as she climbed into her car, she hoped nothing had happened to him and that he would come back to work soon.

***

Driving along Collier Street, Marya took a right onto Route 17 which would take her toward the South Myrtle Beach area. Dorcas Wood having turned out to be such a prickly harridan, she felt she owed it to herself to check out some of the other martial art schools along the coast. She had seen several listed in the phone book and hoped she might find one she liked just as well, one whose master didn't hate her.

An hour later her mouth and mind were curved into a bow of disappointment. One worn, unkempt school of karate had proven unacceptable. The art of karate was not her discipline, anyway. A more likely candidate had been a small t'ai chi ch'uan school, but she decided t'ai chi, the art of moving meditation, would have to wait until she mastered the highest taekwondo belt.

Master Wood's, it seemed, was the only studio which adhered to the same martial art philosophy she did. She saw martial art training as a way of life, a path of self-improvement that must, pretty much, be traveled alone. Tournament competition was fine for some if that was what their own personal path encompassed, but it was not her way. She preferred the path of solitude, of quiet accomplishment under a master's tutelage. Trophies meant nothing to her, and every studio she had entered thus far had displayed trophies indicating competition as a measure of their worth.

Why couldn't Master Wood be more agreeable? Obviously she and Marya held to the same philosophy. The framed pictures in Dorry's lobby had portrayed that same private path of personal growth that Marya believed in. Why did Dorry have to hate her so? She wondered about this hatred, especially as it related to her status as a master. Shouldn't Dorry be past that type of tawdry emotion? Deep inside she recognized the fact that masters were as human as their students, but shouldn't someone who had trained so long and hard that she had won a black belt of rank many times over be able to set aside her feelings and train her with equanimity?

Her outlook brightened suddenly. Of course she should! This was not her problem to deal with; this was something that Dorry needed to work through. Marya knew then that the right thing to do was to return to Master Wood's *dojang* and work as hard as possible following her own path. Dorry would come to see her as an ally eventually—because she would prove herself to her.

Full of new purpose, she decided to turn around and go home. As she pulled to one side, her eye was caught by a large window advertisement featuring a *dobok*-wearing taekwondo artist executing a high sidekick. The neon sign above the building read *Barnes Taekwondo* in tall red letters. Seeing no trophies in the window, she decided to stop one last time.

A smiling man with a blond crew cut and wearing a white taekwondo tunic greeted her just inside the door.

"Can I help you, miss?" His tone was polite, but somehow she sensed sarcasm beneath his politeness.

"Yes, I'm interested in training in taekwondo. What type of programs do you offer?"

"How old is your son?" he asked, eyes examining her curiously.

"Oh, I don't have a son. This is for me."

He paused a long moment.

"Well, we have a six-week sign-up session just starting. It's a hundred forty-nine dollars to join. Then if you want tournament training, sparring, like that, it's an added sixty and you have to buy all your own gear."

"I'm not interested in sparring," she said when a lull fell in his dialogue.

He smiled widely, "I didn't think so, but I'm supposed to tell that to everyone, even the women who come in. I suppose you'll want to try the class for a week or so before you decide whether you want to sign up for the long course, right?"

His patronizing smirk was getting under her skin in a major way, and she could feel her cursed Irish temper getting the better of her.

"Look here, you cretin," she said in a low voice, her tone steely but still under control. "I wouldn't take your blasted class if you were the last school in a nuclear holocaust world. Your attitude toward women is appalling."

Her voice had risen against her will, and an older man, a master wearing a dark blue *dobok*, appeared in the *dojang* entryway. He studied the situation for a moment, then spoke, his voice commanding. "Thomas, what is going on here?"

Thomas bowed his head and gestured respectfully to the master. "The lady is seeking instruction, sir!"

The master's gaze traveled to her face, and his deep brown eyes impaled her. She bowed and extended her hand.

"Marya Brock, sir."

He took her hand and returned her bow. "Fred Barnes. A pleasure to meet you."

An awkward silence fell, then Barnes spoke. "You seek instruction in the way of hand and foot?"

"Yes, sir, but I am afraid our paths differ. I hope you will excuse my intrusion."

She glared at Thomas and moved toward the door.

"Please, Miss Brock." Barnes's voice arrested her. "Forgive my student. Obviously he has had a poor teacher. It is simply this; not many females come through our *dojang*. Those who do are very young and do not usually stay. This has colored our perception of women in the martial art."

She moved closer. "Then how do you explain a master such as Dorcas Wood? I mean, look what she has accomplished. She even has her own school."

Barnes's back stiffened noticeably, and he drew in a sharp breath of air. "You know Dorcas Wood?" His eyes studied her unmercifully. "How do you know her?"

Marya backed off, confused by his vehemence. "I was going to train under her but I...I wanted to see other schools first."

He nodded and closed his eyes. Thomas watched his master cautiously, his mien unaccountably nervous.

"She is a good teacher," Barnes said finally as he slowly opened his eyes. "You would do well in her school. Many women go there and are pleased by her method."

Another long silence fell.

"Please excuse me now," Barnes whispered. "I must... return to my class. Thomas, you will assist me."

The two men left and Marya stood alone, thoroughly puzzled by the encounter.

CHAPTER SIXTEEN

Fortifying herself with the reminder that Master Wood's antagonistic feelings toward her were not her problem, she approached The Way of Hand and Foot *dojang* Wednesday evening. She was nervous. It had been a long time since she had entered a new school, and she longed for the familiar, comforting faces of her old *dojang*. Making the best of the situation, she entered the lobby with her head held high.

She found the women's changing room within minutes and slipped from her street clothes into her practice uniform. The feel of the soft, comfortable, very worn material centered her. She began to look forward to a good workout. Carrying her belt loosely in her hand, she bowed and stepped into the *dojang*, the carpet rough on her bare feet.

Several students, mostly lower belt ranks since they were the remnants of an earlier class, stood about the practice area. Many were stretching, others stood in small groups talking. She sought a deserted corner and after tying her belt around her waist, began stretching muscles that had been wearied by a day of sitting at a desk.

"Hi there. You're new."

A young woman had suddenly appeared before Marya. She was a brown belt, one ranking below Marya's, and she carried herself with the self-confidence of an experienced student. She smiled and extended her hand, bowing in the traditional taekwondo manner. Marya returned the smile and with a bow, took her hand firmly in hers.

"I'm Marya Brock," she told her, "from Seattle, Washington."

"You're a long way from home, Marya Brock," the student said, her eyes twinkling with merriment. "Karen Jenkins, from right here in good old Schuyler Point."

She released Marya's hand and clasped her own hands behind her back, her legs spread in the relaxed stylized posture of the martial artist.

"So what brings you to the East Coast, Marya?"

Marya studied her, noting the glossy sleekness of her long, dark hair and the brightness of her gray eyes. She was very attractive. "Well, I guess I needed a change. And my parents live here."

"Oh, you're living with them?"

"Yes. Well, I was, but I just moved into a new place a few weeks ago. It's over on Begaman Cove."

Karen nodded. "That must be near Master Wood's house. She lives over there. Have you met her yet?" She studied Marya calmly.

"Yes, yes, I have, but..."

"Let's line up, please!"

Marya jumped nervously as Dorry's authoritative voice echoed across the *dojang*. She had entered the practice area from behind her, and chills jittered along Marya's spine as she imagined those cold blue eyes raking across her back. Warily, she turned and caught Dorry's gaze. The master was unreadable, her face impassive, her eyes icy as she glanced away to watch younger students scurry from the room.

Karen grasped her numb fingers and gave them a squeeze. "We'll talk more later," she whispered as she pulled Marya into line.

There were just eleven students in this high-ranking class. Because they were well-trained, they joined the line as though materializing from thin air. Marya glanced along the line, noting that most were close to her age except for one teenager who had already acquired his first belt.

"I see we have a new student. Karen, since it seems you have already met her, perhaps you would like to make the introductions," Dorry said, her gaze resting on anything but Marya.

Karen stepped forward one pace. "I'd like to introduce Marya Brock from Seattle, Washington, sir!" she announced in a crisp voice.

She stepped back into line, and the whole class as one unit turned toward Marya and bowed in welcome. When Master Wood turned her eyes upon her, they were as cold as ever.

"Welcome to our *dojang*, Marya. We hope you will find balance and peace with us."

Marya bowed, deliberately dropping her gaze to the floor. Though it was subtle, she knew Dorry would understand and accept the message. In class she would always be subservient to her. All their differences were to be forgotten once she passed inside the doors of the *dojang*. When she raised her head, she saw Dorry's eyes soften in acceptance, then the master inclined her head in a small nod of understanding.

Classes under Master Wood were much the same as those in Seattle under Master Hayes, comprised mostly of powerful kicking and hand-arm strike exercises. They worked together well as a class. Marya was paired with Karen in tumbling and sparring work.

Later Dorry moved the entire class together in the *kebong* form. Marya was impressed with the quality of the students' performance. Even the youngest and oldest of them moved through the graceful stylized defense moves with near-perfect form. Obviously Master Wood spent a lot of time and energy with her classes.

At the end of the ninety-minute workout Marya was winded, but her body was glowing with vitality. She smiled at Karen as they walked to the changing room together.

"That was a good class," Marya told Karen as she slipped out of her uniform trousers and into a pair of sweatpants. "What type of master is she?"

"Master Wood? She's a great teacher. I worry about her, though. She seems to have no life other than this school. I mean she's here almost all the time."

Karen, already dressed in T-shirt and jeans, was brushing her long hair.

"Why? Is she the only instructor?"

"Oh no, she's got at least three belts she has trained. I guess she has a hard time delegating authority or maybe she's just bored, not an uncommon occurrence here in Marstown."

Marya chuckled and stabbed at her own hair with a brush. "What? With an exciting mecca like Myrtle Beach nearby?"

"It gets old quick, believe me. Listen, I always go to Sissies after class for a milkshake. Would you like to join me?"

Marya eyed Karen's placid face and stuffed her uniform into her gym bag. "Sure, that would be great."

***

Dorry watched Karen and Marya leave the parking lot and an unwanted trickle of jealousy ran through her. As if she had any claim on the girl. Or wanted one.

She turned from the window and reared back in her office chair. She wove her fingers together over her hard belly, the hands looking extremely white against the black of her *dobok*. She studied the desk blotter, letting her mind drift.

Marya. "Star of the sea." Seeing her on the deck of her Begaman Cove property, Dorry could believe she was indeed a star from the sea. A bright gift left there for Dorry. A gift she wanted to claim, she admitted to herself at last. For the first time in a very long time, she wanted to lay claim to someone. To Marya Brock.

She sighed and shifted her eyes, gazing blindly at the many framed plaques and certificates of accomplishment that peppered her walls.

Marya Brock.

It had been good to see her in class earlier. Too good. This had Dorry worried. She found Marya attractive, but there was no way she could be in a relationship. Not in this town. She would have to move away, give up her business, give up her life here in Schuyler Point. She could not allow the public here access to her private life ever again. Which meant the skinny redhead was off limits. Dorry would not, could not, choose her over the life she'd built from a good measure of tough forbearance as well as years of blood, sweat and tears.

A sound penetrated the silence. Her phone was vibrating. She snatched it from the desk and eyed the caller ID. She grunted absently. It had been a while since she'd heard from him. He knew better. He was not allowed, by law, to contact her or get within one hundred feet of her. She was tempted, just from curiosity, to pick up the call, but doing so might encourage him. If there was one thing this caller did not need, it was encouragement.

She replaced the phone on the desk, ignoring the call and putting her old friend from her mind. She thought instead about an old love. Isabel's call had unsettled her. No matter how hard she tried to get her out of her mind, all she had to do was hear her voice and all bets were off.

She dreaded the emotional upheaval she would experience upon seeing Izzie again, but curiosity was eating at her; she wanted to find out what was plaguing her.

Dorry closed her eyes and allowed herself to remember how it had been between them, how their combined chemistry had set them afire. A heat kindled between Dorry's thighs as she relived those moments of passion. She saw candlelight. Saw the pale blush of frothy champagne, the drink that had always been Izzie's favorite. Saw her hands smooth their way along long, slender legs as she kissed her way up along one flank. Rising, she looked deeply into eyes that gazed lovingly back at her. Watched the deep blue eyes close in pleasure, pale lashes feathering against freckled cheeks, as she lowered her face for a kiss.

Dorry rose on shaky legs, her heart leaping in her chest. She strode to the door, pausing at the portal to try to regain her composure. The legs she had been caressing had not been the tanned ones she knew so well. They had been pale. And freckled. And God forbid, those had not been Isabel's eyes. Izzie's eyes were brown.

Dorry staggered along the hallway and into the *dojang*. The room was empty but chaotic with scattered equipment. With a frenzy born of desperation, Dorry started putting things away, hoping the chores would force Marya's sensual image from her mind.

CHAPTER SEVENTEEN

"A reporter, huh? I thought your name sounded familiar. I saw one of your stories this past week. You write well."

"Thank you," Marya replied as she pulled the paper wrapper off her straw.

Sissies turned out to be a small diner fronting on one of the small side streets in Marstown. The proprietor, aptly named Sissie, was a loud, boisterous woman who delighted in reciting riddles to see who in the dining room could guess the answer. The atmosphere was relaxed and jovial. Marya decided to be a frequent customer.

As Karen had promised, the milkshakes were excellent. Since Marya had missed dinner, she also had a salad and an order of french fries. The food was delicious; the salad was even loaded with fresh veggies. "I'm afraid others do not share your love of journalism."

Karen frowned. "What do you mean? Has someone been bothering you about your writing?"

"No." She shook her head, feeling foolish for having brought up the subject. "It's just before I knew how Master Wood felt about reporters and the media, I was goaded into asking her for a story. Big mistake, let me tell you."

"I can imagine," Karen commiserated, nodding her head as she sucked loudly at her milkshake. "Ever since that Francie Rose thing, Dorry has really avoided the press."

"Francie Rose?" Marya's ears leapt to attention on either side of her head. "What's that all about?"

"Oh," Karen leaned forward eagerly. "You don't know about that, do you?"

She shook her head and settled in for a story.

"Francie Rose used to live with Dorry in the house Dorry lives in now. The two of them got together in this small town in Germany, though I think their families already knew one another. See, Dorry grew up here and her family has always had that big place on the cove. They were pretty well off, Texas oil, I believe, even though they've been here a while. Anyway, she was traveling through Europe and stopped in to stay with Francie's father and mother who were stationed there. After they bounced around England and France together, Dorry brought Francie back here and put her through school. I think her dad wanted her to graduate here or something, because she did."

"How old was she?"

"Dorry or Francie?" Karen screwed up her brow as she asked the question.

"Both, I suppose," Marya said, shrugging.

"Well, Dorry was in her…forties, I guess, and Francie, though she was young by US standards, started her senior year in high school here. She graduated from Schuyler Point that year."

"How long ago was that?" She figured Dorry had to be pushing fifty.

"About eight, ten years. But this is where it gets sticky. Francie got sick a few months after she graduated and, of course, Dorry took her to the best doctors. It turns out she had this bad type of cancer. Dorry changed a lot during that time, according to my mother. She used to be this real reckless-type person, always laughing and doing stupid things. Well, after Francie got sick, Dorry became a recluse and spent every day taking care of her. Francie went through all kinds of treatments, but she just got sicker and sicker. I think she held on for like three months until one night she just died in her sleep."

"God, how tragic," Marya gasped. Her heart swelled with sadness. "What a horrible thing to have happen."

"Wait, you don't know the whole story. See, Francie's dad, who had originally consented to let Dorry care for Francie so she could attend school here, all of a sudden changed his attitude. He decided Master Wood was this lecherous old lesbian who had put the moves on Francie and seduced her away from her parents. He went public with it, and the story was on TV and in *People* magazine, lots of places. Oh, it was terrible. Poor Master Wood couldn't show her face without some reporter shoving a microphone or a notepad down her throat."

"So that's why she's the way she is," Marya mused. "I can't really blame her."

Karen nodded. "Yeah, it was pretty awful. I was too young and self-absorbed to remember most of it but I've heard people in my family talking about it."

"So, do you think it was true?" She dropped her eyes trying to be nonchalant although her heart was pounding furiously.

"What? That's she's a lesbian? I really don't know. She's never been married or been associated with anyone else other than Francie, so could be. Maybe they *were* lovers."

Marya eyed her closely. "Does that bother you?"

Karen recoiled, a frown etched onto her features. "Gosh, no! Even though I've never thought about it too much. I mean, I really don't care what she does. She's an excellent teacher and that's all I care about."

"I'm sure others aren't as charitable as you." Marya turned her face away.

Karen agreed ruefully, her chin propped in the palm of one hand. "Yeah, she had a hard time. Most people just ignored old man Rose, especially toward the end when he got so weird and moved back up North with his wife. I'm sure a few of the good old boys here still give her a hard time though. Maybe that's another reason why she stayed with the martial art; so she could defend herself."

"That may be."

Silence fell between them. Marya was glad that she finally learned the story of Dorry's life, but she felt like an intruder, as if she had pried into a place forbidden to her. After a few moments she changed the subject, asking Karen about her life and career.

"Me? I'm just a cashier, over in Myrtle," she said, shaking her head with a frown.

"*Just* a cashier?" Marya smiled at her, amused by the description.

"Well," she began slowly, "I do go to the community college…studying art. My mom and dad aren't thrilled but that's okay. I just love graphic art. I want to be in advertising someday."

"Way cool," Marya responded. "There's always a need for that. Your parents should look on it as job security."

"It's the whole starving artist thing, I'm thinking. How could I ever be financially successful at something I really enjoy?"

Marya nodded her understanding. She munched the last of her crispy fries while Karen told her about her boyfriend, who was an expert with computers. They had gotten engaged a few months ago, and she had been allowing a preoccupation with wedding plans to sabotage her artistic career.

As she listened to Karen talk, Marya quivered inside. The thought of Dorry being a lesbian like her filled her with unreasonable joy even as her heart sank. It wasn't as if Dorry would ever be her friend or a confidante. She could barely tolerate being her taekwondo instructor.

"Hey, how does a witch know what time it is?" Sissie leaned across the back of their booth. "Do you guys know?"

Karen grinned and shrugged her shoulders. "No idea, Sissie. How does a witch know what time it is?"

"I'll handle this," Marya said grandly, motioning for Karen to back off. She used her paper napkin and slowly wiped her hands before speaking. "I'll bet she looks at her witch watch, right?"

Sissie laughed and slapped the back of the booth. "Right you are, she looks at her witch watch. Get it? Witch watch."

Karen screwed up her face in distaste. "Yeah, Sissie. We got it."

Still chortling at her own wit, Sissie moved away. Marya lifted one questioning eyebrow to Karen.

"It was probably drugs," Karen explained in a whisper as they rose to leave. "She's a child of the sixties."

Marya looked at Sissie, dancing behind the counter in her flat sandals and cobalt blue waitress uniform, wild brown hair escaping various confinements.

She nodded as they moved toward the door. "Yep."

CHAPTER EIGHTEEN

He seemed to have gotten smaller. Mama swore she was feeding him, but I wondered. Maybe it was because he was in that huge metal dog crate, though I would have thought it would make him look bigger.

I sat and watched him a long time. Until he started to squirm and look at me with those washed-out angry eyes.

"Are you hungry?" I asked finally.

"What do you care?" he said, his voice raspy and quiet. "You and your mother are both crazy. I can't wait until y'all are found out and have to pay the piper."

He looked at me, his gray hair messy and laying limp on his forehead. I saw where he had sweated through his shirt in several places. Mama had taken his tie and his belt, and his clothes hung loose on his thin body. He looked like a scarecrow.

"Yeah, it's hot in here," I whispered.

I stood and nodded. "Could be. Could be we're crazy. Could be we'll get caught for stealing you. Not much I can do about that now. Is it?"

His mouth flapped open and closed a few times, like he was getting ready to say something. After much effort, words came out.

"What I want to know is how y'all kept it secret for so long. Didn't anyone put two and two together?"

I noticed how dirty and disorganized the cellar had become. The man's water cup had toppled. I fetched a cloth from a nearby shelf and started mopping up.

"Just no sense in anybody being such a slob," I muttered. "I just don't understand why people can't do things the right way."

He leaned forward, wrapping his fingers through the crossbars of the cage. His knuckles were white from the force of his fingers pressing against the diamond-shaped holes in the wire. "Which means your way, right?"

I studied him, twisting the cloth in my hands. "Maybe. What's it to you?"

"So what's your name, anyway? The one you go by."

"Puddintane. Ask me again and I'll tell you the same." The old rhyme made me smile.

"Bat shit crazy," he muttered.

I had tried to be nice, but I had had just about enough of his mouth. I moved as fast as I could and slammed my palms against his fingers, pinning them to the metal with my body weight.

He screamed as much in fear as in pain, it seemed, and exhilaration raced through me. I'd show him crazy.

Inserting my own fingers through the holes of the metal fencing, I grasped his middle finger and pulled it as far through the fencing as possible then pressed backward. The clean snap of the broken bone was immensely satisfying, and I closed my eyes to better savor it. Opening them seconds later, I watched his eyes, saw him struggle not to scream again. Hatred flared in his eyes for a brief moment, and I studied it, pleased that I had caused such an emotional response.

I cooed at him as I let his hand go. He cradled the hand to his chest, and I saw beads of sweat pool on his broad forehead. One pool overflowed, and droplets scurried along his cheeks.

I stood and strolled away from his cage and began straightening the cellar. I ignored him a long time until he started to speak.

"You're not going to let me live, are you?" he whispered.

I turned and looked at him. His hand must be hurting like a son-of-a-bitch, but he wasn't letting on.

"No, I don't think so," I answered. I folded the cloth I'd used earlier and placed it on the worktable. "Mama says you know too much. That you've been snooping in the computer. What did you find, anyway?"

He watched me, his eyes glazing over some. I guess he was realizing that he was going to die here in this cellar. I didn't expect him to answer so I was surprised when he did.

"Your birth certificate."

"Ahh, that explains a lot," I said, snapping my fingers. "Making that public sure would stir up a tempest in a teapot."

He nodded and scooted toward the back of the crate. He pulled his knees to his chest and continued to hold his wounded hand like it was an infant and he its mother.

"I'm sorry I had to hurt you," I said softly. "Why couldn't you have just ignored that stupid piece of paper? You think I like being bad?"

With his head down, I had a hard time hearing his response. "Because I am a good person and, unlike you and your mother, I know right from wrong. I just wanted to do the right thing."

Angered anew, I decided I'd let him stew for a while.

"Enjoy your pain," I told him as I mounted the wooden steps. I switched off the light and waited a minute. There was no sound from below. He didn't even cry.

CHAPTER NINETEEN

Two nights later Marya was back at The Way of Hand and Foot. The class worked out for a good hour. Marya worked steadily to coax soreness from each of the muscles she had reawakened during the first class. Dorry was a hard taskmaster, but Marya knew the harsh input was improving her form. Dorry's first reprimand—"Spaghetti arms, Brock!"—hadn't set all that well, but, though she had bristled at the correction, Marya had been able to stick to her original promise of subservience in the *dojang*. Per Master Wood's direction, she made a concerted effort to sharpen her angles. She did it at first to avoid further embarrassment in front of the class, but soon afterward realized she was doing it because she had come to respect Dorry's opinion and value her approval.

In time, Marya was able to set aside how daunting she found Dorry's presence, as well as the feeling that Dorry hated her, and find bliss in the regular workouts and forms that taekwondo offered. The loss of self was the reason she had stayed with the martial art for so many years. It was good to find that again.

As Kim's betrayal began to fade from her mind, she could feel the real stirrings of a new life. She thought about dating. She would start soon, she decided, but as yet she had not found anyone who sparked her interest. The free tabloids that peppered the sidewalk outside her grocery store often listed a gay and lesbian club in Myrtle Beach. She'd check it out as soon as she was more settled.

Lost in thoughts of attractive, oh-so-welcoming lesbians, she started when she heard her name called by Master Wood. She stopped her repetitive kicks to the leather punching bag and swung wide eyes Master Wood's way. What had she done now?

Dorry stood next to the mats, hands clasped behind her back, scowling at her.

"Brock!"

Marya gulped and hurried over, panting as much from fear as from exertion.

"Yes, sir!" she postured stiffly in front of Master Wood, heart racing.

She saw one of the twenty-somethings approach, a young man named Rob Tyler. The two of them had developed a nodding acquaintance, and she nodded to him now as he stepped onto the mat. He stood across from her, and they both eyed Dorry expectantly.

She cleared her throat and stepped off the mat. "Tyler attack, Brock, defend. *Hapkido*, please."

She handed Rob a protective breastplate as Marya's mouth fell open in surprise. *Hapkido*?

"Not linear," Dorry explained as if reading her thoughts. "*Hwa* first."

Ahh, nonresistance. With great effort, Marya relaxed her body, a task made extremely difficult by the fact that she had spent the previous hour pumping her muscles into a state of tension. Next she relaxed her mind, draining the force from it as she watched Rob don his protective gear. She knew from her *hapkido* training that when practicing the *hwa* form, the mind must be as relaxed as the body.

When Rob was ready and moved toward her, Marya felt his energy meet her chest, but she moved back, to one side. With a flick of her right arm, she allowed him to twist until he spun forcibly into the space she had occupied. He tumbled head over heels once, then rested supine on the mat. He raised his head and looked at her from the confines of his padded helmet.

"Again," barked Dorry, who was watching at the edge of the mat.

Rob rose and rushed her again, but just as he was about to meet Marya, Dorry shouted, "*Weon.*"

Marya immediately allowed energy and force to rush in and fill her. She shifted to the right and grabbed Rob by shoulder and elbow. She spun him in a circle, using centrifugal force and the momentum of her body to fling him away from her. The force carried him so far that he landed off the mat and slid across the wooden floor, knocking down a trio of students as if they were bowling pins. Amid the ensuing chaos, Dorry's voice rang out:

"Again! *Yu* form, fist first."

Rob leapt to his feet and charged at Marya from across the room. As his feet hit the mat, he uttered a guttural cry and his fist lifted above his head. Marya let loose her own power cry as she engulfed his fist in both her hands and allowed the length of his arm to penetrate between her own outstretched arms. She shifted her body and the threat of bone breakage took him down to the mat where she knelt on his chest even as she held his outstretched arm taut in a stranglehold.

"*Sool,*" Dorry muttered. "Tyler, try to escape."

Rob twisted, his movements tightening the grip Marya had on his arm. She eased a bit and allowed him to pull free but dug her fingertips into the soft shoulder tissue beneath his rotator cuff and pinned his other arm to the floor with her forearm. He yelped in pain so she eased off, but he was completely incapacitated by the grapple hold. She closed her eyes, not wanting to see his pain as she waited for the release order. Dorry barked it and she fell back onto the mat, releasing Rob completely. He sat up and massaged his shoulder.

"This is true *hapkido*. It kills if left unchecked and used for ill. Is this the power you wish to have, Tyler?" Dorry asked softly.

"I outweigh her twice over," he muttered in amazement, looking at Dorry. "Can you really teach this form?"

"Yes," Dorry nodded, "but I think Miss Brock might be a better teacher for you. Is this what you need to learn?"

Rob looked at her, and Marya could see him weighing options in his mind. She wondered how he would use the art, whether for good or bad.

"I'm being bullied," he explained to Marya as he pulled up his *dobok* to show her an old bruise that still glowered along the side of his lower abdomen.

She nodded to him and then nodded to Dorry. "I will teach enough for defense," she stated firmly.

"See me after class," Dorry told her. "Dismissed."

Marya rose and left the mat area to cool down. Letting her mind ramble, she ran through several of the early form *poomses*. She was amazed that Dorry thought her good enough, and responsible enough, to teach another student the *hapkido* forms. A small part of her thrilled, but she was also nervous. She didn't want to let Master Wood down.

***

Later, waiting in Master Wood's office, dressed in her street clothes, Marya felt at a distinct disadvantage. As

Master Wood talked with another student just outside the door, she studied the things Dorry surrounded herself with. The first thing that snared her attention was a large basket just to the right of her desk. It was full of brightly colored stuffed animals, colored pictures and envelopes. She leaned forward and realized that they were gifts given to Dorry by her students. Many of the animals still had bright cards and banners of gratitude attached.

The wall behind her desk was covered in shelves. On them she saw rank after rank of taekwondo books as well as many books from other disciplines. Most of them appeared well worn. She knew somehow that Dorry knew well the information contained inside them. The shelves were also peppered with metal trophies and photos of a younger, smiling Dorry accepting those trophies and certificates. There was even one of her being presented with a key to the city.

Marya spied a photo of a woman who bore a striking resemblance to Master Wood and another in which this same woman sat next to a younger, smiling Denton Hyde. Curiouser and curiouser. Obviously Dorry and Denton knew one another well.

Spotting an aged photo of a pleasant-looking older couple, she wanted desperately to go over for a closer look. She knew better, though: As soon as she stood, Dorry would come in, catch her snooping and become angry with her anew. But Marya was nosy. Was this a photo of her parents? What had happened to them?

The door opened and Dorry entered. She sat at the desk across from her and fiddled with a stack of folders that rested to one side. The chair squeaked as she sat back and regarded Marya.

"You're doing well," she said, with no preamble. "I believe Rob will do well under your tutelage. How do you feel about it?"

Marya cleared her throat and clenched the light jacket resting across her lap even tighter. "As I said, I have no problem teaching him defense only."

Master Wood nodded and studied the hand she had resting on the desk. "I think if he thwarts one attack powerfully, there will be no more."

She looked up questioningly at Marya.

"I agree," she said, looking away, wanting the discussion to end.

"So shall we say six weeks of training?"

Marya looked back at Dorry, questions and doubts bumper-car-ing within her mind. "Yes," she answered finally.

"Good," she replied, reaching into a desk drawer and drawing forth a business-sized checkbook. "The fee for specialty classes is one hundred twenty-five dollars. Twenty-five goes to the *dojang* and one hundred comes to you. Do you find that satisfactory?"

Marya sat as if shell-shocked. Was Dorry offering her a job? Working here, with her? She glanced up and realized she had fallen silent. She could see the flickers of irritation beginning to crease Dorry's forehead.

"Yes, yes," she answered hastily. "More than generous."

Dorry scribbled in the checkbook and handed her a check for the hundred. Marya held it in her hands, her feelings and mind numb.

Master Wood rummaged around and found a small piece of paper that she also handed to Marya. "This is his contact information. Please get in touch with him and set up your own scheduling."

She fell silent, and Marya studied the words written on the note. They were in block letters, and the strokes forming the letters reminded Marya of elegant Japanese calligraphy. Realizing the silence had stretched on too long, Marya glanced up to find Dorry holding a single key strung on a The Way of Hand and Foot logoed keychain. Dorry was looking down at it, frowning doubtfully. Sensing Marya's interest, she placed the key gently atop the desk and, using one finger, pushed it toward her.

"This is to the side door. Rob knows to come in that way for sessions after hours. Please keep the front doors closed when you are teaching and lock the side door securely when you leave."

Marya understood Master Wood's concern, above and beyond mere business concerns. Though Marstown was a low-crime area, there were no doubt those who would deliberately seek to harm Dorry and/or her livelihood.

"I will," Marya told her. "I promise."

Dorry looked up at her and their gazes locked briefly. "Dismissed," she said quietly.

Marya stood and moved to the door but felt Master Wood's eyes on her back. The gaze was tangible, as powerful as a caress, and her breath hitched in her throat. She paused, knowing she had to speak to break that intense moment of connection.

"Dorry," she began slowly. "Thank you."

Marya could sense that Dorry understood why she was really thanking her—for trusting her. Dorry's voice, when it came to Marya, was low and rich and almost seductive in tone. "You're welcome."

Marya made her way out finally, afraid to look back.

CHAPTER TWENTY

"Still no Denton," Ed stated the next morning. He frowned at her as though she were personally responsible for keeping Denton from his work.

"Well," she began helplessly, adding nondairy creamer to temper the bitter office coffee. "Has anyone gone by his house to check on him? Maybe he's hurt and needs help."

He frowned even harder, if such a thing were possible. "Of course. I've been by there three times and he's never home. His car isn't there either. I even looked through the garage window. No car."

Marya was unsure how to respond, but a nibble of fear started rumbling in her solar plexus. "Seriously, do you think he's having a midlife crisis or something? Did he go away?"

Ed poured coffee into a huge tumbler and added copious amounts of sugar. "I don't know, but he'd better have a damn good excuse for being gone this long is all I have to say."

"Has he done this before?" She sipped the tepid coffee and ingested a globule of undissolved creamer. Ugh.

He shook his head and leaned his upper body across the break room counter, his weight supported on his forearms, one hand cradling his mug. "No, only when his wife died, which, of course, was understandable enough. I told him to take all the time he needed then. He was gone three days then, and it's been more than that now."

Marya was perplexed. She didn't know Denton that well, but she recognized his attention to detail and sense of duty, common to most journalists. Being irresponsibly absent just didn't seem part of his nature.

"He'll be back soon," she said with conviction. "I'm sure of it."

"Who are you trying to convince?" Ed said, eyeing her with a sideways glance. "You or me?"

She sighed and shrugged. "Both of us, I'm thinking."

"I'm not convinced," he answered with his own heavy sigh as he straightened his back. "If I don't hear from him by the end of today, I am calling the police in the morning. I don't care how much trouble it causes him."

She nodded in accord. "I agree. Listen, I finished his proofreading on the A-front and I'll jet it over to you as soon as I boot up."

"Thanks, Marya. I don't think we'd make a single deadline if not for your help."

"No problem, Ed. Like you, I just want him back here."

She left Ed and moseyed to Denton's desk as she sipped her coffee and tried to dull her offended taste buds. If not for the caffeine content, she wouldn't touch the stuff. She had dropped her backpack by the desk earlier. Now she switched on Denton's work station. The computer desktop waited, blinking at her as if impatient. She was reminded of the robot, Number Five, in the film *Short Circuit*. The comical one who was always saying, "Need input!" Smiling to herself, she sat down and gave this machine input, typing in the generic *Schuyler Times* login.

She dug down into her bag and pulled out the bright blue thumb drive on which she had stored Denton's proofreading files. Deluged at work, she had taken the A-front home last night to make sure she made deadline today. She plugged it in and waited for the machine to recognize it, then dragged the A-front file folder to the desktop. When no replacement window popped up, she leaned forward and examined the desktop. The original file was gone. *What the hell?*

Everything else seemed to be there, even the silly folder of plant catalog orders she had brought over the day before. She used the search function to find the A-front, thinking she had erroneously placed it into another folder. Nope. The folder was gone.

A sudden chill rushed through her. She knew she had had the folder on the desktop when she left work yesterday. She distinctly remembered checking for it after copying it to the thumb drive. Very weird. Had someone been in Denton's computer?

She glanced around to see if anyone was watching. She keenly remembered the Dorry interview episode and knew her co-workers weren't beyond a good practical joke. Was she being punked again? No one seemed to be giving her undue attention.

Had there been some sort of server failure? She checked other files and folders again, making sure all the regular desktop shortcuts were still directing properly.

Everything seemed to be okay, but worried, she tapped the waste bin icon and scrolled through the items there by date. A folder called "Private" was the next to last one deleted, just before the A-front folder. Following a hunch, she dragged the "Private" folder back to the desktop and then onto the thumb drive. She also copied it to her personal file that was kept on the *Schuyler Times's* server before deleting it again. There was no real reason she could cite for feeling like it was important to do this, rather she was following her gut—something that had helped her before in her journalism career.

Putting the folder from her mind, she put the final touches on the A-front files and then sent them over to Ed via interoffice e-mail. She stretched, leaned back in her chair and glanced around the office. Marvin had come in and was talking on his phone, one hand idly twirling a pencil as he studied the loafer-clad feet he had propped up on his desk. Dallas was at her desk as well, scribbling on a yellow legal pad, reading glasses perched on the end of her nose. Connie stood at the layout table at the back of the pasteup room, visible through the wide doorway. She was laying out ads, a ruler and X-Acto knife protruding through the fingers of her left hand as her right sought the perfect placement. Marya could hear the faint soul music that Wallace and Craig often played.

Looking to the front, she saw Carol dutifully working on some filing at the reception desk. Over to her left Ed was studying his computer screen, peering like an owl through his glasses, and Emily was filing her nails with keen attention as she talked on her phone. Everything seemed so normal. Yet someone—one of these people, the ones with access to Denton's computer—had taken a folder and then tried to sabotage the paper by deleting the A-front files. A bad feeling began to churn in the back of Marya's mind.

CHAPTER TWENTY-ONE

On Thursday, Marya was able to take a day off from the *Schuyler Times*, a rare opportunity given that Denton was still missing. Ed had reported his disappearance to the sheriff's office the previous morning and the day had been a tedious waiting one, full of meetings and questions as the police investigated.

Wanting to use this special day well and seriously needing a nature break, Marya made plans to explore the land adjacent to her small cottage. Household chores, laundry, weeding the flower gardens and mowing the small patch of grass took longer than expected so she got a late start. After tucking a water bottle and snacks into a small pack, she donned hiking boots and set off.

The weather was delightful. At eighty-five degrees, it was just hot enough without being too hot. The low sun rested heavy on her face as she blazed a trail through young pine trees. She headed into the wooded area, avoiding the beach where she might encounter Dorry. Dorry's house was east of the wooded area, and she had no desire to let an impromptu sparring match with her dampen the peace and contentment of the day.

The woods were surprisingly cool due to the shading of the interlaced tree branches overhead, and she found herself shivering in her thin T-shirt and shorts. Mosquitoes buzzed around her head and a few biting flies nipped at her knees. Nevertheless she was happy, her legs falling easily into the pumping rhythm of the hike, her breath rate increasing. Squirrels scampered at her approach, and small tribes of nut-brown quail made frantic escapes as she passed. She found her footsteps following the natural curve of the land as it sloped upward.

At one point she had a wonderful view of the rental cottage with the mighty surging sea as a backdrop. She admired the neat square of lawn over which she had labored just an hour before, proud of the result. The many small, bordered flower gardens formed fascinating geometric patterns from this vantage, and she was sure that they were much more attractive without the choking green of the weeds she had removed earlier that day.

Marya plowed deeper into the forested acreage, eventually emerging into a natural clearing. The warm sun kissed her in greeting and she strode the perimeter of the small sandy lot. White cotton clouds passed overhead and she stood, head thrown back, feeling vertigo as earth and sky rubbed against one another. Dropping her gaze, she spied a patch of blue through the trees on her right and moved forward. The blue was the ocean and she could see a house. Master Wood's house.

Larger than she remembered, it was a lovely home when framed against the ocean, with shutters and trim of deep blue. The siding was a weathered white and the sloping driveway, made of creamy crushed stone, blended in well as it framed the property. The house settled onto a thick, half-moon shaped peninsula of rock which jutted out into the water so its foundation was regularly caressed by frothy waves. The backyard sloped down to a dock and a landing where a small boat stirred restlessly at its mooring.

Feeling a sense of guilt, even though she wasn't intentionally spying, she turned away and returned to the clearing. Settling herself on a patch of soft sand, she sipped water and thought about Dorry. She forced herself to think of Dorry's positive attributes, her strength, her bold attractiveness, her determination to make her mark in a traditionally male-dominated discipline. Still, the image of her blue eyes flashing in fury kept intruding.

Marya forced all thought from her mind then, falling with practiced ease into that state of no thought, of the nothing that is the everything sought so often by Buddhist monks and practitioners of the martial art.

Sometime later she allowed full consciousness to re-enter and came back to herself feeling refreshed and years younger. It always amazed her how energizing meditation could be. Though her legs were stiff from being folded for what seemed like hours, she could feel each mentally revived muscle fiber better than before. Her mind was quiet, oxygenated, her thoughts slow and crystal clear.

Stirring reluctantly, as dusk was fast overtaking the land, she took a hearty drink of water, then began a casual stroll toward home. Realizing that she was lost in the trees, she began slanting her feet toward the ocean. The number of trees decreased and the last fading rays of slanting sunlight helped guide her steps. Soon she spotted the beach. Although it was unfamiliar, not the beach below her home, it was a welcome sight.

She had emerged into the tree line just behind Dorry's house, she saw. She prayed Dorry wouldn't see her. She was feeling too good for another battle with the woman; it would ruin her pleasant mood. Then she saw Dorry. Her next indrawn breath nearly choked her.

Dorry was swimming toward her across a small, enclosed pool of ocean water. Her muscular arms moved with smooth, powerful strokes, her short, white hair turned silver by the water. Marya stepped back so she was hidden by trees and watched her, hypnotized.

Dorry climbed into the shallows below her deck and rose up, strong hands sluicing sheets of water from her suit-clad form. Marya was amazed by the richness of Dorry's body—her breasts were melon globes of rounded flesh. They swelled from a hard muscular chest and were topped by visible nipples centered in the bodice of the crimson suit she wore. Her shoulders were broad and curved with muscle and her wide belly lay flat and smooth. Her legs rose like columns of sculpted granite, meeting with curious grace to cup the dark shadows at the mount of Venus.

After scratching idly at her right thigh, she turned and dove into the deeper water, hands cupping and pulling her through the salt-water pool with dynamic speed.

Marya was too shaken by the sight of her to complete her passage along the beach. She had to turn away and melt into the trees. Traveling just inside the line of trees along the beach, she made her way home.

Once inside the cottage, she mechanically fixed hot tea. Only when the cup was in front of her on the kitchen table did she allow her mind to focus on what she had seen and, more importantly, on what she had felt.

Marya desired Dorcas Wood in a big way. Watching her unconscious casualness had affected her in a strange fashion. She'd seen her share of half-dressed females in her life—males too, for that matter. So why should the sight of Dorry affect her so? She reviewed her feelings.

How much of this was due to what she had learned the other evening? Was she enamored of Dorry just because she now knew she might be a lesbian?

What was most amazing to her was the way her body had reacted. She reached one hand down and pressed it over the mound of her sex, able to gauge wetness even through the fabric of shorts and panties. A gentle throbbing still disturbed her there. She brought her hands up, swept them across her breasts. Her nipples, awake and alert, leapt to new life beneath her palms.

She drew her hands away and shuddered. She wanted Dorry. The feeling rushed across and through her. She imagined Dorry's wet sleekness pressed against her, Dorry's taut, wet skin sliding over her own. She ached to heft the heady fullness of Dorry's breasts in her hands, wanted to pluck the ripe red raspberry nipples from them with her lips. She wanted to plunder the crevice of Dorry's sex with her fingers and tongue. She wanted these things with an ache that was consuming her entire body.

With a growl of frustration Marya left the table, her tea untouched. She crept to her bed as if suffering a dire illness and crawled beneath the blankets, assuming a fetal curl, both hands pressed to her groin. There she stayed, eventually falling asleep, her mind trying to understand that awful, puzzling ache that was consuming her.

Several hours later she awoke, her eyes wet with tears, the roar of the ocean surrounding her. The cottage was hot, so she kicked the coverlet aside. Her thoughts flew to Dorry as she came fully awake. How could she be so enamored of a woman who hated her? She knew then that her subconscious tears were for the futility of her situation. She told herself that Dorry would be no different than the rest of the women she'd temporarily shared her life with and been disappointed by. Surely she was doomed for even more disappointment as the barriers to touching Dorry's soul and spirit loomed even larger.

Yet, there was something there, some unspoken something between them that had begun nagging at Marya a little more every day. She recognized it as attraction and it scared her. She didn't feel equipped to deal with the growing feelings she was developing for Dorry. She didn't feel she could handle the resultant regret of forcing them to go away.

She rose and strode into the night through the front door.

She watched the ocean for a time, then walked around back to lean one hip against the railing and watch the full moon as it lolled above the trees. The moon glow made the night transform into the murky crispness of a developing print; certain surfaces were raised in bas-relief while others retreated into light and shadow. She wrapped her arms about herself in a comforting hug. She so wanted to have someone in her life, but she would rather be alone than with a prickly pear of a woman who was incapable of tenderness.

It was at times like this—after seeing Dorry's intriguing beauty—that she realized how lonely she had allowed herself to become. She had told her mother she wanted closeness, touching, tenderness. Was it out there and she just wasn't capable of seeing it? Or had she been blind to it on purpose, afraid of finding what she thought she wanted and discovering it still wasn't enough? That *she* still wasn't enough?

She thought of the women she'd loved, listing them on one hand, considering why the relationships had foundered. It was not always her fault, she decided, at least not totally. They lost steam, just weren't meant to be. There was someone out there for her. She still believed that. She had to. Someone who could touch her in places she'd never been touched. The question was, when the time came, would she allow them in?

She watched the bright, rotund moon for a long time, telling the silent psychologist all her problems, all her dreams. Then, just as she turned to go inside, she spied it; a light oblong of fabric at the base of a tree about ten or twelve feet into the forest, a new addition to the familiar landscape.

Curious, she walked across the deck, her slippered footsteps resounding too loud in the quiet night, even when she moved from echoing wood to the soft susurrus of leafy litter. Two minutes later she realized what she was seeing.

Her mind tried to lie, actually argued with her eyes about what they saw. But there was no denying it. A dead body lay crumpled at the base of a small pine. And though she wanted so badly to disbelieve it, she knew by the distorted, blackened face gazing heavenward that the lifeless form belonged to Denton Hyde.

CHAPTER TWENTY-TWO

Inspector Christopher March was a small, neat whippet of a man whose dynamic energy whirled like a tornado in her small, calm kitchen. Marya was relieved when he settled that energy into the chair opposite her.

She watched him dully, her senses still chilled by finding Denton in the forest.

"So, Miss Brock. I'm very sorry you've had such a disagreeable experience this morning. I know it must have been grim being the one to find the body."

"Yes, I'd say it was grim."

His strong cologne made her nauseous. It had that strange gingery smell which she had never liked.

"I saw him in the trees from the porch because the moon was so bright. I thought he was a pile of clothing at first. I would have missed him entirely if not for the moon."

He was watching her with eyes full of judgment and doubt. It seemed as though every word she said was being evaluated for merit and judged for credibility. He was weighing every fact she shared against what he knew to be true and therefore gospel. The tension made her uncomfortable, which was no doubt his intention.

The door swung open and a familiar face below a blond crew cut entered the kitchen. She was trying to remember who the man was, and her shift in attention caused Inspector March's head to swivel.

"Hello, Thomas." March said and her memory jarred. It was Thomas, the rude belt from the Barnes *dojang*. And he was a deputy sheriff for Coburn County. Lovely. "Canvass the rooms here and I think we'll be through."

Thomas's eyes swept across her, amusement in their depths, and she felt soiled by his consideration. He moved off into her home, meandering, hands clasped behind his back.

"So tell me, what were you doing out on the porch at one in the morning?" The inspector's intensity had returned to Marya.

"Why is that important?" she asked, bristling with annoyance. "I couldn't sleep. I have a lot on my mind."

"Ummhmm." He leaned forward, elbows on knees. "How long have you known Mr. Hyde?"

"Me? Less than a month. I only knew him from the paper, the *Schuyler Times*. We both work there." Her eyes were following Thomas. She was praying he wouldn't touch anything.

"And would you say your relationship was amicable? Did you get along?"

"Of course. I like Denton. He's a teddy bear of a man, sweet and shy. And he knows everything there is to know about a newspaper." She gulped, still unable to believe that precious life had been snuffed out like some insomniac's morning candle. "Did know," she amended quietly.

The whippet was trying to be sympathetic, but she could sense his impatience. She realized he was waiting for her to mess up, to drop a clue that she was guilty in some nefarious way. He probably carried that attitude throughout his life. Marya bet his wife cringed every time he asked why his eggs were scrambled instead of fried.

"Ummhmm. And how was the body when you found it?"

"Just the way it was when your men got here. I didn't move him. I didn't even get real close. As soon as I realized what it was, I called nine-one-one."

He watched her in silence until it became uncomfortable. "How well do you know Dorcas Wood?" he barked finally.

The change of subject startled her. "Not well at all."

Her mind flashed to the image of Dorry swimming in the pool below her house, and she knew from the flush on her cheeks that her face had to be mirroring some of her thoughts. She cursed the fairness of her Irish skin. "I met her about a month ago. I rent from her."

"And take lessons? In karate?"

How could he know so much about her? There's nothing like a small town for disseminating information. She felt violated. "Taekwondo. And yes, three nights a week."

"So you've been studying for quite some time?"

"Yes, many years."

His eyes flew to her worn purple cloth belt, resting on the coffee table in a sinister looking S shape. "Purple belt, huh? Can you break a board with your hands? I saw that on TV once."

Marya frowned. "Of course, cinderblocks too. What has that got to…"

Marya fell silent. How had Denton died? Gunshot? She hadn't seen any blood. Suppose Dorry had…no, it was too horrible to contemplate. The inspector was speaking and Marya tried to focus on his words.

"Dorry's good. I've seen her compete a few times. She's very strong." He was watching her closely.

Marya swallowed, the dry sound a loud click in her ear. "Yes, she is. And she's a good teacher, as well."

Again he nodded, a low sound of assent issuing from his throat. He looked around the cottage, sharp eyes missing nothing. "You live here alone, don't you?"

"Yes, I just moved here from Seattle to be near my parents but wanted a place of my own."

She knew what he was implying, but she wasn't about to help him along with it. He wanted real hard to believe that Dorry and Marya were sexually involved and that Denton had stumbled upon it and become a victim of their illicit passion. After all, Dorry was the town lesbian and a dangerous martial artist. What great gossip to share at the old police water fountain.

"So you're what? Divorced?"

She stared evenly into his eyes, daring him to step onto this molten ground. "No, never married. Guess no one could tolerate me for the long haul. A reporter's life is pretty busy and we stay preoccupied with our work."

"Yet you had the day off yesterday, I understand."

She turned her face away so he could not see the flare of anger brightening her eyes. "Yes, sometimes I take a day off."

"And you did...*what* all day?"

She turned cool eyes back onto him. "I don't think that is any of your business."

Thomas's radio sparked into life and he strode out the door. She wanted to sing hymns of thankfulness. Now if only the whippet would leave.

March smiled, as if happy she had flared up at last. "Now, Miss Brock, this is a murder investigation. I think it has to be my business."

She was determined to maintain her equilibrium so she smiled back at him. "That's true and in the spirit of cooperation, I will tell you that I cleaned and mowed my yard, then went for a long walk in the woods. I sat in a clearing at the top for a long time, most of the afternoon, then walked back home just after dusk. I fell asleep early and that may be why I woke up at one o'clock."

He watched her, eyes blinking rapidly. "Sat in a clearing. Were you alone?"

She shrugged. "Afraid so. I told you, no one can stand me for the long haul."

"Right." He sighed and stood. "I think I have everything I need, Miss Brock. I'll be in touch as information develops. Do you plan on staying in Schuyler Point?"

"Sure. Like I said, I moved here to be close to my parents."

He nodded and walked to the door, eyes roving across the main room of the cottage, searching for last-minute clues. This was one man who took his job seriously.

Just a little more than an hour later all the blue flashing lights and busy voices were gone from the area around the cottage. Marya had been sitting at the table the entire time, watching the first phase of the investigative process in action. Another cup of tea in a long series of cups sat chilling before her.

She had not called her parents. She was not crazy about the idea of them knowing Denton's body had appeared practically on her doorstep. With a sigh, she admitted to herself that this was just the beginning of a long road of trouble that she had no desire to deal with.

She hadn't called Ed either, though she knew she should have. She didn't know his home phone number, which was a good excuse, but she could have left a message at the paper. She found herself unable to imagine how she would explain what happened and why it had been in her yard. And no doubt Ed would badger her about writing the story herself later in the day, something she just wasn't ready to deal with quite yet.

Marya yawned in spite of her troubled mind and realized just how tired she was. She glanced out at the sun brightening the sky just to the right of the bay. Ed and the crew were just going to have to survive without old Brocklyn this day. She grimaced, betting they would all know why anyway. The police blotter would see to that.

Her reporter mind went into action and she found herself pondering Denton's death and what good thing it could have provided for anyone. What could be the motive for his murder? Did he have money? Was it revenge? Jealousy? She played over all the stock motives and none seemed to fit. Maybe he was just in the wrong place at the wrong time.

She thought of the young people she had encountered her first day in Marstown, remembering that Dorry said they were often on her property. Were they harmless? She remembered her sense of unease as they surrounded her.

Wearily she rose and switched down the ringer volume on her cell phone. She was positive she'd be grateful for that later, although she wasn't sure she'd be able to sleep. She walked to the door and peered through the side window in the direction Denton's body had lain. Yellow police tape had created a maze in the small portion of the forest she could see from that vantage point. She believed herself absurdly safe now that it was daylight and knew she might be able to sleep after all. If truth be told, she was pretty tired of thinking about the whole mess.

She turned toward her bed, shaking out sheets left rumpled from her earlier nap. As she lifted one knee to the mattress, however, something hit the braided rug that rested beneath the bed, landing with a solid thunk. Curious, she bent to fetch it and found herself holding a heavy gold link bracelet with a satin-finished, brass plate attached. She leaned into the first golden rays of sunlight slanting from the kitchen door and saw the word Dorcas engraved in cursive writing across the front. There was a small diamond just to the right of the last letter. She hefted the piece in her palm as she pondered possibilities. Had Dorry been here last night? The bracelet couldn't have been in the bed earlier. She would have felt it, wouldn't she?

New worry nagged at her. Was she in danger? Had someone—Dorry—been in her house? She gripped the bracelet in her hand and moved to the door to double-check the locks. The kitchen windows were open for air but had screens accessible only from inside. Someone would have to cut them to gain access and she would hear it. Heart thudding, she moved back to the bed and pulled the sheets around her. She curled on her side and stared at the bracelet in her hand.

CHAPTER TWENTY-THREE

Marya's desk was a cluttered mess. She moved the piles of waiting paper firmly to one side. She had to find some tangible means of proving her innocence or it could come down to her word against that of the Coburn County Police Department. She was definitely not yet considered one of the locals, and around here outsiders attracted finger-pointing like magnets attracted iron. It didn't look good. Especially not with deputy-dog, misogynist, smart-ass Thomas involved.

Marvin had intimated as much during his hour-long interview with her. Off the record, of course. Though Marya had offered to do the story, Ed had refused, saying it was a front-page piece. Marvin's beat, not hers. She knew the real reason; he wasn't one hundred percent sure she wasn't involved somehow.

At least her parents believed her. But they also believed she was in harm's way, her mother begging her to move back in with them until the investigation was over and the bad guy caught. Marya sighed as she tucked her bag under the desk. Her mother hovering over her twenty-four/seven? Not a chance.

Who did murder Denton? Who could be heartless enough to do away with such a sweet old soul? Her mind raced across possibilities and raged like a brush fire gone wild.

Snapping on her computer, she found solace in old friends—the national police database and the national news archives. These were familiar stomping grounds.

She entered codes and passwords until she came to the Federal Bureau of Investigation. Her reporter status gave her only limited access. Still their database might provide something useful. She typed in Denton Hyde and waited, the fingertips of her right hand smoothing the knuckles of her left.

His name was there but not as a criminal.

In 1996, in Richmond, Virginia, he had witnessed a purse snatching, fought off the perpetrator and reclaimed the bag. The bad guy had gotten away, but Denton had been fingerprinted. Witnesses and victims often were, so their fingerprints could be ruled out during investigations. Nothing in the file indicated a possible motive for his murder. It held other information, though, including his wife's maiden name, Darlene Wood. This had to be Dorry's sister, the woman whose photo she had seen in Dorry's office. Denton once told her that cancer had taken his wife too early. She sensed that Denton had never quite gotten over her death. Could there be some grain of motive there? Could Dorry have taken Denton's life as payback for some past transgression? Certainly she had the power, the physical strength, to snap his neck, and temper enough. Marya had seen evidence of that.

But Marya had also interviewed a few confessed murderers. They had all had a sort of devious sullenness about them, magnified by a moment-by-moment intensity that disconcerted everyone who knew them intimately. Dorry seemed different: She didn't seem jaded by life or agitated by it. She just wasn't...interested. She seemed as though she were fed up with it and the paltry pearls it had to offer.

So, if not Dorry, who? She leaned back in her chair and wove her fingers into a tiny blanket across her abdomen. A drifter? A random incident? Murders were rare here, Ed said, even with the town's proximity to the much larger area of Myrtle Beach. Still, she'd seen some reprehensible characters around, gathered together outside some of the bars along the major highway between Marstown and Myrtle Beach. A drifter was a definite possibility.

A chill passed through her. How close had the killer been to her? She sat upright and studied the newspaper she'd called up from the dead files.

Lower down in one article she saw a small grainy photo of Francine Rose. She looked very young, much younger than seventeen years. Her face was waif-like, reminding Marya of a burgeoning Audrey Hepburn. Even her hairstyle, worn long but drawn into a high, thick ponytail on the back of her head, reminded her of Hepburn. She found herself being drawn to the girl by the simple sweetness of her expression.

Reading the article, she discovered the charges against Dorry had been brought by Francine's father, Nicholas Rose. The story was ludicrous, every "fact" raised against Dorry a circumstantial one. Dorry was neglectful because she didn't rush his daughter to the hospital at the first sign of the cancer that killed her—a low-grade fever lasting more than a week?

Anger seethed through her soul as she examined subsequent issues of the paper. How dare this imbecile do this to Dorry? His ploy may not have been evident to all, but it was clear to her with her reporter's background. Knowing his accusations wouldn't stick, Rose had tried to ruin Dorry's reputation and to destroy her business. In a town as small as Marstown accusations of lesbianism and neglect could easily do that.

She studied the photos taken of Dorry at that time. They showed a woman on the edge but gritting her teeth and digging in her heels to avoid being dragged over the precipice. Admiration nibbled at the edges of Marya's anger. She was proud of Dorry for standing strong.

Finally, after more than eighteen months of follow-up stories, in which expert medical testimony played a large part, Dorry was exonerated. A jury found her not liable in the death of Francine Rose.

"Ha!" she muttered, "I bet that scorched old Nicholas's ass but good!"

"You talkin' to me?" Dallas peered at her from two desks over. She was looking over the top of her reading glasses and her comical expression coaxed a smile from Marya.

"Nope, just myself. Hey, what do you know about that Dorry Wood case? The one where her ward died?"

"Why do you want to know?" she asked with avid interest. "What do you want to know?"

"Well, I think the whole thing was a farce," she responded. "Imagine bringing trumped-up, impossible charges like that against her just to ruin her reputation."

"Hmmm," Dallas moved closer, one hand smoothing the eyeglasses sprawled on her chest. They looked like some symbiotic, alien insect that had taken her over. "A man in grief is likely to do anything, you know. I certainly can understand why Nicky brought the charges. Francie was his world. The only reason he allowed Dorry to keep her here was so she could go to school here and be safe while he and Isabel trotted all over Europe. When she got sick and died, he was a mess. Then he found out about the, well, unnatural nature of their relationship and all hell broke loose."

Marya watched Dallas, whose hand was twirling a battered pencil like a baton. "How well did you know Nicholas?"

"Oh, he was part of our little group," she revealed, sharing a bright smile. "We were all very close. See, Dorry, Dolly, Emily, Freddy, Nicky and I were all at Coburn High together. We graduated together and then most of us went to the same college."

"Freddy?" Marya lifted one finger in question.

"Barnes."

"So that was how Dorry knew Nicholas."

"Well, yes, the families had been friends forever," Dallas confided. "We all used to go hiking and get together for holidays, play cards, that type of thing. We were all together until Nicky went into the military and was sent to Germany for some type of special training. He met Isabel there and then we just didn't see him anymore."

"He dropped all his friends? Now he really sounds like a jerk."

Dallas was taken aback. "Oh no, it wasn't like that. He's a good man and people do part. You know, life interferes. A big part of it is just her, that wife. She had no time for us."

The sharp edge to her voice set off alarms in Marya, especially after the earlier sweetness of her tone. "What do you mean?"

"Isabel. All of us knew why he went with her. She just swept Nicky off his feet, that's all. She's so polished, so... European...and her family has gobs of money. We really couldn't blame him. Then they had Francie and he fell head over heels in love with his little girl."

Marya studied Dallas, noting a curious, bright cast to her eyes. Sadness filled her. Clearly, Dallas lived vicariously through other people. "And you, Dorry and Emily never even married," she prompted softly, her eyes shifting toward Emily's office.

"Well, not because Emily and I are like Dorry," Dallas responded, her mouth pursed primly. "It's just Marstown and the pickings are pretty slim, let me tell you..." She smiled wanly and Marya saw the Dallas she had known the past few weeks. "Well, back to it. The social news waits for no one," Dallas chirped, settling her eyeglass insect back on the bridge of her nose.

"Yeah," Marya agreed, turning her attention back to the computer. She raised one querying eyebrow at the display monitor. Dallas, Emily, Fred, Dorry and Nicholas, barbeque buddies right here in good old Marstown. Well, well, well.

CHAPTER TWENTY-FOUR

Driving home that evening, fatigued from pulling double duty as well as doing her own private research, Marya pushed back at the fear that threatened to encroach. The beautiful home that had once seemed so secure and serene, had been forever scarred by Denton's murder. Police tape, loosely encircling the trees, gleamed in the soft moonlight, twisting in the ocean wind.

Pulling her car into the parking area, she switched off the engine and lights and sat silent a long time. Waves, white and sparkling in the dusk, slapped with teasing play against the ruddy shoreline.

She was tired, so very, very tired. So much had happened so fast—moving to Schuyler Point, working hard to get up to speed at the paper, resuming classes, finding Denton's body. She leaned back in the driver's seat, laying her head to one side. The ocean was beautiful, lit by a narrowing corona of light. Marya loved this time of day. So quiet, so still, as if everything were saying a final goodnight. How she would have enjoyed Kim by her side—the old Kim, not the person she had become before the split. She shook her head. She was not delusional; she knew that was not possible. And anyway, overall, this solitude fit nicely. She sank into it.

After some time she stirred herself, sensing that she'd fall asleep if she stayed put. Her legs carried her to the porch with reluctance; she trod each step laboriously, ascending slowly.

"About time you got here, murderer. I knew you'd return sooner or later."

Marya recoiled and stared up at Dorry. The master was sitting just to the right of the front door on a weathered wooden bench built into the porch. She was leaning against the wall, one heel propped on the edge of the seat. She had yet to look at Marya. Her face, which was turned seaward, looked desolate, but the sarcasm in her voice pushed away any tender feelings the view might have fostered in Marya.

"What do you mean, murderer?" she asked sharply. "I'm not responsible for Denton's murder. I'm the one who called the police, remember?"

Dorry turned a face full of shadows toward her. She shifted position, revealing the bottle of whiskey tucked between her heavy thighs. "Too damn smart, aren't you? Calling the police to direct the blame to someone else. Well, you screwed up, Miss Reporter," she spat the title like a bitter tonic. "Because that someone else was me."

"You've been drinking," Marya said in a neutral tone.

Dorry gave a harsh chuckle, the sound touching Marya in some deep yet intangible way. She lifted the bottle and drank deeply, the bottle glinting in the last light of the day reflecting off the ocean waves.

"Yeah, guess so," she agreed, wiping her mouth with her palm.

"Great," Marya said with a sigh. "That's all I need after the past couple days I've had—a drunk on my porch."

"My porch, don't you mean? I happen to own this property."

She was surprised by Dorry's petulance. "Yes, yes, I realize that but, hey, I pay rent..."

"And that gives you the right to murder my family here—because you pay rent!? Oh no, *that* wasn't in the contract we signed."

"Look, it's been my experience that you can't reason with a drunk, so I'm not even going to try," Marya stated with a negating wave of one hand. "I'm going in to go to bed. You stay on out here all night if you wish. It *is* your property."

That said, she strode across the porch and stepped inside. She returned a moment later, her face such a mask of fury that her own skin felt alien. "How could you? I can't believe you are capable of such a horrible act!"

Dorry stared at her a long time, her mind apparently having trouble deciphering her words.

"What's the matter?" Marya said finally. "Too drunk to remember? I knew you were cold, I knew you were calloused, and I almost understand why, but I didn't think you were heartless enough to kill innocent creatures just to get a point across."

Dorry rose on unsteady legs and scowled in irritation. "What are you blathering on about? Kill what creatures?"

Marya searched for signs of subterfuge and could find none in Dorry's disturbed countenance. "The birds. In the house. You didn't do it?"

Dorry's anger was mounting as was her impatience. "Girl, please talk some sense. What birds? Let me see."

Marya stepped aside so Dorry could enter. Inside, Dorry emitted a low whistle of sorrow. "Damn," she said.

Three parakeets had been killed and hung with twine from the chandelier above the dining room table. Their bright colors of yellow and green contrasted painfully with the dead matte of their eyes and pale, parted beaks. They seemed to be watching them with eyes already set on whatever heaven birds could see. Marya's heart hurt every time she looked at the wings partially denuded in their struggle for life.

"Poor darlings," Dorry muttered as she moved to untie them. "We've got to bury them…"

"No!" Marya shook her head wearily. "It's evidence. We need to call the police. They can search for fingerprints."

She dreaded the thought of dealing with Inspector March again, but it was unavoidable.

"Oh right, lots of fingerprints on a feather," Dorry sneered. "What good will calling the police do?"

"Well, it proves someone else is involved besides the two of us, for beginners. It looks way too much like covering up something if we just bury them."

Dorry placed her arms akimbo, hands on her hips. "Yeah? How? Covering up what? And who else is involved? You've been accusing me of doing it."

"If you didn't do it, and I sure as hell didn't, there has to be someone else involved."

"So says you. I'm taking the poor things down. This is a sacrilege to all that's holy, that's what this is."

She fished a pocketknife from her trouser pocket and began cutting the birds loose. "Imagine someone doing away with them. Heartless butcher."

The angry way she was slashing at the twine alarmed Marya. This woman's temper was fierce. What could she do when thoroughly aroused to anger? The first bird began to fall. Marya reached to catch it just as Dorry did. Their hands clasped together accidentally, precipitating an awkward moment. More troubling than that, however, was the lurch of desire that suddenly jolted Marya.

Images of Dorry swimming, embedded indelibly in her mind, chose this moment to come to the forefront. With a sharp, indrawn breath, she shut her eyes, allowing the inescapable sensations to swamp her. When she opened them, Dorry was there, close, and she was watching her.

An eternity passed as they gazed at one another, their hands together still. Unbelievably, she saw Dorry's eyes change, become tender, and the blue more dense—filled with a kind of easy passion that she had never seen on anyone before. Her face changed too, losing the tense lines of barrier that Marya was so familiar with. The Dorry that was revealed was younger, more playful and infinitely more lovable.

The moment lasted only a moment, however. Dorry turned away, jerking her hands aside and leaving Marya with only the cool limpness of the dead bird in her hands. Its head drooped to one side, mirroring the deflation she was feeling. A feeling that she now had to swallow and deal with.

In silence, Dorry cut down the other birds, catching each with quick economical movements. They moved in uneasy silence, Dorry wrapping the tiny carcasses in paper towels and Marya untying the twine from the light fixture. Marya could tell that Dorry was as aware of the attraction as she was. But she worried. Was Dorry's attraction true, as true as hers?

She shot a sideways glance Dorry's way as she wrapped the tiny bodies, trying to gauge her mood. Her face was grim. Marya's heart fell. Dorry still hated her and would, no matter the circumstance. The tenderness she'd glimpsed was a fluke, something no doubt caused by the whiskey Dorry had consumed. Marya sighed. It was just as well. Getting involved with Dorry was much more complication than she needed right now.

"I'll get a shovel," she said, hoping the sadness evident in her voice would be attributed to the birds' deaths. "We'll bury them in the trees."

Dorry nodded, staring down at the lifeless bodies. "Good idea," she said, a curious hitch in her voice.

Silent again, they moved through the yard and into the trees, veering left, away from the site where Denton's body had been found. Ghouls on a ghoulish mission, Marya thought.

She dug a shallow hole and Dorry lined up the dead martyrs in a row, yet snuggling them together as if to share warmth. They watched them a long time, Marya secretly hoping they'd stir and fly away, but they remained still. Dorry took the shovel from her hands and covered the poor bodies with a thick layer of dirt, mounding the hole and packing it tight. The two of them spread leaves and litter over the grave in case anyone came snooping.

***

"If you didn't do it, then who did?" Marya asked again as they moved back toward the house. "Didn't you see anyone?"

"No, no one."

"I just don't understand it. First Denton, now this. What is going on? Doesn't it seem like it's some type of personal vendetta against me?"

"Or me," Dorry replied quietly.

"Yes, or you. Any idea why?"

Dorry shook her head and laid one arm across the stair railing on the front porch. She seemed lost in thought and very sad. "I can't fathom it either. I can't say I much like thinking about it."

Childish fingers of ocean wind played with their hair and clothing and then gleefully ran away.

"You know, it was different here when I was a girl. People knew their places then and could accept themselves. Now they're aimless and looking for trouble. I see them every day at my class, young boys coming in thinking that the fight is what it's all about. They forget—or refuse to learn—that we study the martial art so we won't fight."

Marya nodded, remembering the same words coming from Master Hayes at her old school.

They watched the night ocean without further conversation. Dorry's statement was a lot, coming as it did from a woman who feared no silence, who even welcomed it. Marya was soothed by the stillness that created. Too often when people were together, they felt a need to fill the silence between them, whatever the cost. She and Dorry had no such agenda, none of that tension. Realizing that filled her with relief.

An owl hooted in a faraway tree, giving her permission to voice her curiosity. "Assuming you didn't kill Denton—and knowing that I didn't—you have any idea who might have?" The bird echoed her query softly, its own plaintive who-who carried away by ocean sylphs as they passed by its perch.

Dorry turned shadowed eyes on her. They moved across her like a warm caress of wind during a desert twilight. The tilt of Dorry's head almost caused Marya to stop breathing. The threat of danger rested heavy upon her. What would she do if Dorry were a murderer?

"I can't believe he's gone. I would have done anything to protect him. If I'd only known he was in danger…"

Marya's interest was piqued, but she wanted to act circumspectly, knowing that sharing her feelings like this was difficult for Dorry. "Danger? From whom? What do you know?"

"Nothing really," Dorry sighed as she leaned her shoulder against the porch railing. "I have guesses, theories, nothing concrete."

"Will you share them with me?"

"Why? So you can get a good story? Scoop everyone else?"

Her attitude was beginning to piss Marya off. She moved closer, getting in Dorry's face, trying to make her hear her.

"Look, Dorry, I may be a reporter but it's just a job, okay? I once made the mistake of confusing my job and my life but never again."

With her face just inches from Dorry's now, it would have been such a simple thing to lay her lips on hers. To kiss her easy and slow, a kiss of healing and truce. She almost did. Then their eyes met. Passion ignited, burning in slow licks of fire across her torso.

Marya pulled back and continued in a shaky voice. "What we're facing is serious. We could be in trouble if Denton's real killer isn't found and soon. This has nothing to do with getting a story; it's all about you and me not becoming a tragic statistic. Now, are we going to work together on this or am I on my own?"

The ultimatum was clear. Marya could see Dorry mulling it over.

"But, it's not so easy..." Dorry turned and pressed her forehead to one of the porch uprights. "When I'm with you..."

"What?" Marya leapt upon her words. Did she feel something for her? Did she?

"I just get so incredibly angry at what and who you are. It's hard for me to get past that."

Sudden, surprising tears filled Marya's eyes, and an involuntary sob escaped her. She turned away so Dorry wouldn't see the tears, hoping to be able to examine the painful feelings those words had spawned in her.

"Marya," Dorry said, turning attention her way. "You okay?"

Marya swallowed her sorrow and replaced it with fury, which was more familiar, less threatening. "Listen, anger or no anger, we have to deal with this. If you know anything about the murder then I need you to tell me about it. It's only fair since my ass seems to be on the line just as surely as yours."

Dorry was taken aback by her vehemence. Seeing that gave Marya a momentary flash of satisfaction. She also hated her in that moment.

Dorry walked away with purpose. Marya feared she would leave. She stopped fifty paces away, arms wrapped about her own shoulders, and stared at the ocean. Marya watched as the fretful wind caressed her, envying it, regretting that she would never have that opportunity. Life could be so unfair.

Maybe coming to Schuyler Point had been a mistake after all. She longed for the security of Seattle. There at least she knew her friends…and her enemies.

"I think it's those kids, the ones I ran off the beach that night. They're hooligans. They could have done it. An accident, probably."

"No, it couldn't be. None of them are strong enough…"

Dorry turned and rushed toward her. Marya cowered, filled with a pure, reactionary fear.

"How can you be so sure?" Dorry choked out. "Denny was small. Dolly used to call him her little banty rooster."

She smiled sadly and pressed both palms to her cheeks, scrubbing at her eyes. "Look, I'm going home. I'm so tired of all this crap."

Marya called her name softly as she turned to go. She looked back over her shoulder and their eyes met. Dorry's sadness wailed through her…and then she was gone.

CHAPTER TWENTY-FIVE

"Talking to yourself?" Ed asked from behind Marya.

She hit the minimize key on her keyboard and turned to greet him. "No, not really. Just thinking out loud, I guess."

"Hmm." He slipped one hip onto the far corner of her desk and swung a raised leather-clad foot with thoughtful mien. "It's okay to talk to yourself, I hear. It's the answering you have to worry about."

Marya smiled and shook her head in amusement. "Oh, really?"

"So, what are you working on?"

She noted that his expensive leather loafers were scuffed and pulling apart at the seams. Ed was a true newshound.

Little mattered but the next story. "I'm just entering Denton's stuff and working on that dog piece you gave me. Why?"

"Just wanted to tell you that Sheriff Gennis called me. He had a bunch of questions about you and Denton. I reassured him you didn't off Denton just to get his job."

"Well, thank you, I guess." Marya watched Ed. She wondered…was he guilty…trying to frame Dorry?

"They don't really have anything on you, you know." He looked away and then back, eying her with concern. "It's just because you are new here."

"Oh, I know," she assured him quickly. "I understand that."

"Well, I wanted to make sure all this mess didn't sour you on Marstown. We're good people here. This thing with Denton…well…" He took a deep breath and let it out slowly. "It's just bad business. First murder we've had since '72 when the Sully boy did in his girlfriend, Teresa, and her new lover."

"I sure do miss him," Marya said softly.

"Shoot!" exclaimed Ed, frowning. "Me too! Him and me been friends for fifteen years. Life just isn't the same without him here."

His eyes slid to Denton's desk and visited briefly. Maybe he wasn't the murderer. Or he was filled with guilt.

"What was Darlene like?"

Ed shrugged. "Sweet lady. Grandmotherly type, even though they were never able to have children. She really would have been a good mother too. Always making cookies and bringing them around. She loved to share a good funny tale…had a new one every time I saw her. You know, she made a birthday cake for each of us every year. And threw a little party for us."

Marya wanted to ask whether her temperament had been like Dorry's but was uncomfortable suddenly. There was one thing she could ask.

"Ed, you know a lot about this community. Who do *you* think killed him? Who would do such a thing?"

Ed looked at her as if surprised by the question. "Oh, it had to be someone from out of town. No one from Marstown could do such a thing. We all loved and respected Denny. I don't expect we'll ever find out who really did it. Whoever it is...he's probably long gone by now."

Standing, Ed wandered off to chide the intern who was scattering archived issues on the workroom counter. Marya was sorry to see him go. She would have loved to ask him more about Dorry's possible involvement, to see just how far he would go in accusing her. After the night before, after the time they'd spent together cloaked by the South Carolina evening, Marya was having a hard time believing in Dorry's guilt. She wanted to see if Ed concurred.

Tapping the mouse, she brought up the *Times* database and dragged the "Private" folder she had stashed there onto her desktop. She glanced over her shoulder to make sure no one was nearby and then clicked the folder to open it.

The blasted folder was empty. Marya sighed, disappointed. She had hoped—and expected—it would shed some light on the mystery surrounding Denton's death.

***

The next two days were quiet, filled with work and with contemplating the changes occurring in her life. Not that everyday life had changed; it was more a shift in the person that she was—or thought she had been. Thoughts of Dorry worried at her every moment she wasn't working, and that rarefied time just before sleep descended each night was filled with erotic imaginings of the two of them together.

Which was ridiculous, really, since the Dorry Marya knew could never be capable of the intense intimacy her imagination had conjured up.

Yet the feelings persisted. She became a walking picture of arousal, her body constantly moist and aching for Dorry's touch. She hated this betrayal. The least her body and mind could do was lust after someone accessible. Surely, it was some cosmic joke that she should desire the most unattainable, yet most intriguing, woman in Marstown.

Compounding her woes was the vision of dead birds with sightless eyes and limp necks that haunted her sleep when it finally came, robbing her of desperately needed rest. So it was with jaundiced eyes and a less than amenable nature that she faced Saturday morning's assignment, covering the annual Schuyler Point Rescue Squad fund-raiser. Marya was uneasy about leaving the house as well, fearing finding another unwelcome surprise upon her return. Realizing that making a living had to take priority over fear, she locked the house as securely as possible and made her way out into the South Carolina sunshine.

The fund-raiser, a picnic and mini-carnival, was held at the Amlyn Community Fairgrounds, no more than ten minutes from her home. The festival was well underway by the time she arrived and she merged into the crowd, notebook in hand. She jotted down a few first impressions to give the readers a sense of what the event was like, then began listing the fund-raising participants. Marya knew she would obtain a complete list from the organizers, but she liked to note her own impressions of the more outstanding booths. Many of the local businesses had come out to help the rescue squad, and she obtained a wonderful quote from Sammy Long, owner of a video store downtown, about how the rescue unit had been there within minutes the time he almost died from a heart attack.

The pickings were easy and soon she was able to take a well-deserved break with a soda and a bean taco at a wooden bench in a small grove of trees. The biting flies and mosquitoes were having a heyday but it didn't bother her much. Her mind was churning, racing back and forth between her notes about the fund-raiser and possible motives for Denton's murder. It just didn't make sense.

Dorry, the more she came to know her, didn't seem as much a suspect as she once had been. Seeing her tenderness with the birds had given her a better understanding of her as a person. Randomly harming anyone or anything just didn't seem a part of her nature, no matter how the evidence looked. She might have some unknown reason to hate Denton, but if she followed the belief system displayed in her *dojang*, it was impossible, ludicrous even, to imagine her heartlessly torturing and killing him. So who?

Her eyes roamed across the mass of people before her, judging and weighing possibilities. Her eyes fell upon Dallas, busy serving sodas at the Ruritan booth. She seemed such a friendly little woman, but Marya had seen the bitterness and jealousy she harbored about other people's lives. She wasn't big enough or strong enough to kill Denton the way he'd been killed, though.

Ed Bush passed by with his petite, plump wife Louise, giving her a wave and an approving nod. She'd heard from him and others about his longstanding feud with Dorry over the Francie story. Would he have done anything so heinous as to murder Denton just to frame Dorry? She didn't think so, but she'd been fooled before during her years as a reporter.

Karen sat on a nearby bench engaged in an intimate conversation with, she assumed, her boyfriend. He was handsome, with a bookish air about him; they were a well-matched couple physically. She envied them their closeness and the sweetness of their interlocked gazes as he rose and walked away. Shifting her attention away from him, Karen spotted Marya. Her face brightened and she made her way over to Marya's table. She was in her uniform, something that was normally worn only in the *dojang* or in competition. Suddenly Marya understood Karen's attire, remembering that there was going to be an exhibition of taekwondo on the festival stage. Had she already performed?

"Hey, Marya, how are you?"

"Fine, wishing I were home."

"Oh, pshaw," Karen said, perching on the bench opposite Marya. "It's a beautiful day and there's such a good turnout. I'm glad to see it too. It's about the only way the rescue squad can finance what they do."

She paused and studied Marya, taking in her haggard appearance. "You're not sleeping much, are you?"

"No, not really. I found dead birds hanging in my house the other day. It's creepy there now."

Karen gasped, then shook her head. "Oh my God, it would do me in for sure, coming upon something like that. Why dead birds?"

"Your guess is as good as mine," Marya answered with a shrug.

They fell silent, watching the activity whirring around them.

"I just hate the fact he's gone. It's so unfair," Marya stated finally, as if in explanation.

"It would be one thing too if he'd gone naturally," Karen said. "But they say he was tortured, maybe beat to death, strangled until his neck broke."

Marya shuddered at the images Karen's words evoked. "Who would do that? Do you know of any enemies he might have had? Anyone who would have a reason to kill him?"

Karen chewed her bottom lip thoughtfully. "Can't think of anyone. Not around here. People just don't commit crimes here the way they do other places. It's such a small town that everyone knows everyone else. People pass through, but they usually never stay long enough to cause trouble."

Marya offered no response. Someone had caused trouble this time. Big trouble and she was in the middle of it.

Karen may have sensed her depressing thoughts for she rose abruptly. "I'd better run, Grandma's over there wandering, looking for me, I bet. Listen," she pressed Marya's hand against the worn table in a gesture of caring. "You take care, hear? Don't take any chances. Tell Sheriff Gennis if you see anything else that's strange, okay?"

Marya gave her a tentative smile, touched by her caring. "Sure. Thanks, Karen."

***

As soon as Karen strode away, a new sound emerged from the forested area behind Marya, an urgent whispering that drew her inexorably toward it, her curiosity the powerful cogs on a slowly moving gear.

Tossing lunch residue in a nearby waste bin, she gathered up her notebook and moved into the dense thicket of trees. Careful not to disturb the environment, even by snapping a twig, she was gratified when the whispers continued. As she drew nearer, she began to be able to make out certain words—"danger," which pricked her ears and pulled her ever closer, and "love," another word that ensnared her. She could make out little else, however. Beginning to have qualms about eavesdropping on a private conversation, she turned to go. She was just starting to pull away when she heard a robust "Oh no!" uttered in Dorry's distinctive voice. Dorry was talking to someone under cover of the wooded copse? Did it have something to do with Denton's murder?

Marya held her position, ears straining in the effort to pick up more of the faint voices. She peered through scrub pine branches, poison ivy looping about her bare legs. Then she saw them, identifying Dorry as she was attired in her formal white master's uniform. The woman pleading with her was unfamiliar to Marya but perfectly coiffed and dressed despite the fact that it was a hot day. Her suit was Chanel, her satiny blond hair was twisted into a sleek chignon, and her pumps were spotless, high-quality leather.

Marya could not make out what she was requesting, but Dorry was reacting with her typical impatience, loosening the woman's hands from her forearm and shaking her head vehemently in the negative. Finally the woman walked off, be-ringed fingers swabbing at her tear-stained face.

Dorry turned her back to the area where the woman had stood; her hands were shaking. The encounter must have been a powerful one. Marya pondered the nature of their relationship. They knew each other well; she could feel the intimacy, argument or no argument. Could they be lovers? The thought gave her a pang.

She moved right as Dorry moved left, emerging onto the edge of The Commons, a wide area reserved for impromptu ball games or community events. Today, groups of karate students were displaying the finer movements of their art for the passing crowd. Always happy to watch martial art in action and needing to be distracted from her disturbing thoughts, she moved to the demonstration area.

Students, few of them familiar to Marya, fought the stylized routines taught in their classes. She was perturbed by the violence she saw manifested by some of the older students. Faces flushed with true anger, they moved to and fro against their opponent as if against a true enemy. She recognized two of them as the boys who had accosted her on the beach her first night in Marstown. One of them, sans his silver ear-to-nose chain, saw her and nodded in a quick, furtive manner. The other youth, the dominant one from the group, did not see her; he was watching his master, Fred Barnes, with intensity. Marya realized why when, at Barnes' subtle signal, he moved in and began a new set of stances. He was a good, forceful leader, quick and focused, though there was a brief flicker of recognition when his eyes scanned on the watching crowd and he spotted her among them.

Barnes, now relieved of his leadership duties, stood by Thomas for a few minutes, then slipped off to one side. Wondering what he was up to, she followed. He seemed to be a good, if competitive, teacher. It puzzled her he could feel and allow so much negativity toward women. She watched as he purchased a bottle of water from one of the many booths peppering the field and took a seat where he could enjoy a slanted view of his students' performances.

Marya approached cautiously, not sure what she wanted to say. Deciding to use work as a handy excuse, she caught his attention.

"Hello, Master Barnes. Your students are doing well today."

He watched her with equanimity. "Hello, Miss. Yes, very well. They've made great strides this year."

"You must be very proud of them."

He eyed her with a *tsk tsk* expression, and she was happy to see that he realized, as did she, that pride had no real place in the art.

"Such as it is," he replied.

She paused a long beat, confused. How could he be one of the true seekers of the art, yet allow such violence among his students? "May I get some information from you?"

He agreed and she began her standard who, what, where, when, why and how spiel, all the while studying this quiet man. He seemed to be so in control of himself, yet she had seen him react emotionally to her mention of Dorry. Was there history between them? And what about the woman Dorry had been talking to? How did she figure into the picture?

Barnes broke off in midsentence, his gaze fixed on the exhibition. The crowd had thinned considerably, not surprising as the day had moved into late afternoon and suppertime, making it easier to see the three young men who were sparring, two his students, the other one his first belt, Thomas. As she watched, Thomas used a cropped back fist blow to bloody one boy's nose. Holding his face, the boy backed off, and Thomas went after the other youth.

It took but a moment for her to realize that he was fighting Ricky, the boldest member of the group that had accosted her that first night in town. Ricky was bigger and tougher than the other student and the fight was more of a challenge. The two had flung off the pads used in the demonstration and the sound of flesh striking flesh penetrated to where she sat. She turned to Master Barnes, expecting outrage, but what she saw instead chilled her heart. An avid look of blood lust lit his gaze as he watched.

A smothered cry sounded as Thomas's shin swept into Ricky's knee. Marya knew the boy would be limping for weeks. She also realized Barnes had no desire to stop the brutality, that he no doubt condoned these true strike altercations in his *dojang*. It dawned on her too, with a smooth epiphany, that Barnes could have killed Denton.

The realization left her dumbfounded. Soon, though, her mind was busy trying to find ways to link the two together, creating scenarios. What connection did they share that could have resulted in Denton's demise? As hard as she tried to move the puzzle pieces around in her mind, however, they would not come together.

"Miss Brock, you will have to excuse me," Barnes said close to her ear.

Marya demurred with polite noises, grateful that he was going to put an end to the sparring at last. To her dismay, however, he just moseyed closer, hands clasped behind his back, and studied the entropic battle from a more intriguing vantage point. Feeling disgusted, she walked away.

CHAPTER TWENTY-SIX

Fear almost stopped her before she could knock on the door. Marya wasn't sure why the blue of Dorry's eyes daunted her so badly. She had dealt before with bold, strong people like her and had not been so clenched with fear when approaching them. Marya knew without doubt, however, that it would be far worse to continue to stay at home tortured by her imaginings and questions. It was time to get to the bottom of this issue, to learn why her freedom and perhaps even her life were being jeopardized.

She scrubbed at eyes still bleary from the few hours' sleep she'd managed after returning home from the fund-raising picnic. Questions roiling about inside her head had held sleep at bay for far too long and had greeted her upon rising what seemed like minutes later. Nothing had provided relief—soothing music, hot tea, a warm shower. She remained a kaleidoscope of half-formed assumptions, a turmoil of what-ifs. Then a long walk had brought her here. To Dorry's front porch.

Marya strode back and forth on the sea-dampened boards a few times, dreading what was sure to be another confrontation. Her power of choice was whisked away when Dorry opened the door.

They looked at one another a long minute, then Dorry spoke, her voice soft. "You were pretty quiet out here. Not like those ruffians who come by all the time. You have a gentler step."

Marya didn't know what to say, odd for a reporter who knows everyone's business or the right questions to ask to unearth that business. It wasn't often that she was struck dumb. The one person who did it regularly was Dorry. It was a binding under pressure, the result not of having too little to say, but too much. Marya couldn't decide what needed to come first.

"So, out with it," Dorry sighed. "What brings you over here?"

"May I come in?" Marya asked gently. "I want to understand a few things and I believe you are the one who can help me."

Marya was intrigued when Dorry became visibly nervous, hands fidgeting at the bottom of her T-shirt. She reminded Marya of a frightened schoolgirl. What was she hiding?

"I don't claim to understand anything, Marya. Maybe your answers lie elsewhere." Dorry's calm voice belied her nervous gestures.

"Please. I promise I won't stay long."

Dorry moved aside in silence, and Marya stepped into her home. The first sight of the interior overwhelmed her. Candlelight. It was everywhere.

Solar disks filled the floor of the living area. Each contained a rotund center candle with slightly smaller candles that radiated from it in a flickering sunray spiral, but each design was different. Some were Southwestern, others Oriental, some even futuristic. No electric lights were on in the room, but she could see a steady glow in the back part of the house.

Dorry quickly shut the door behind her to stifle the swift ocean wind that threatened the display. She stood with her back pressed against it, studying Marya and her reaction to this unusual offering.

"This is beautiful," Marya breathed. "I burn candles all the time but never thought of doing this."

"Mmm, just a mindfulness exercise," Dorry muttered as she crossed the room to stand at a shimmering wooden bar. She poured golden liquid fire into a glass tumbler and pointed to it to ask if Marya wanted one. Marya nodded and she poured a second.

Marya looked around the room. The house was indeed old but had been painstakingly refurbished, its aged wooden walls and floors stripped and polished to a high gloss. They mirrored the candlelight to such an extent that Marya imagined she was floating in a huge goldfish bowl set atop Dorry's sparkling bar. The illusion was dizzying, yet exhilarating, and she experienced a deep affinity with the forced change of atmosphere.

Marya understood what Dorry meant by mindfulness and why she had taken the time and energy to create the candle patterns. Those who are Zen and study the martial art understand that all life is illusory and that what one makes of life often becomes that life.

Wandering, feeling Dorry's eyes heavy upon her, she walked the circumference of the room, passing in front of the lighted hallway and then back into the ever-moving dimness. She wondered what the real goal was, if there was a goal, for creating this environment. Was it healing, energizing or simply for comfort? She knew that knowing this would give her great insight into Dorry as a person. She couldn't bring herself to ask, even though she craved the intimacy that would allow it. Being this close to Dorry made her breathless, left her thoughts fuzzy and fragmented. She struggled for composure.

"I saw you today...at the fund-raiser. I saw you arguing with a woman. A beautiful woman. Tell me who she is."

Marya turned her request into a gentle demand, raising her chin higher as she looked at Dorry.

"You saw us? Damn you, girl, you're everywhere. Are there no secrets from your prying eyes?" Her steady gaze was filled with admiration as she handed her the tumbler and seated herself on the low sofa.

"I see what I'm meant to see. This charge you and I could face is no joke. I need to know if this woman has anything to do with Denton's murder."

Her eye caught a large wooden frame at that moment. Inside it sat the same woman from the picnic. She was posed and smiling invitingly for the camera—or for Dorry. "Her," she said, pointing. "Who is she?"

Dorry took a sip from her tumbler, as if fortifying herself for what was to come. "I should have known you'd be the one, when I saw you on the beach, your fiery hair a beacon in the house lights. That's what drew me, you know—your hair. I saw it when I stepped onto the porch. There you were sitting there by Isabel's flag just as pretty as you please. I wanted to run you off at first, almost did, but you seemed so sad sitting there and I remembered how I'd sat in that very same spot so many times, by myself, feeling sad and lonely. As if the whole world had just packed up and moved away."

"You feel that way sometimes?" Marya asked quietly.

"Sure." Dorry tilted her head to look at Marya. "And that's the way you looked that night. What were you thinking about?"

"Old loves." Marya dropped her eyes.

"Old loves," Dorry repeated hollowly. "I can tell you about old loves. The woman you saw me with? One of my old loves. Isabel."

The way she said the name made Marya's heart ache viscerally. She glanced at the portrait, still so prominent, and knew the extent of Dorry's love. One had to wonder… did she still feel the same way about her or was there room in her life for someone new?

"I thought…" Marya paused, unsure how to proceed. She moved across the room and sat at the opposite end of the sofa. "Why isn't she here with you?"

Dorry jerked herself to a standing position and walked back to the bar before turning and facing Marya. "Complications. She's married."

"To a man?" Marya stood as well and moved two steps toward her. She paused when she realized she was approaching Dorry and stopped to finger a silver snuff box atop the sideboard.

"Yes. A man who hates me." Her tone was neutral, no emotion evident in it at all.

Suddenly it dawned upon Marya—her second true epiphany of the day. She knew exactly what had happened during that horrible time ten years ago. She lifted her eyes and saw Dorry watching her, the rim of her glass hiding a small, self-deprecating smirk as she took another sip of whiskey.

"You weren't in love with Francie, were you? It was Isabel, her mother, you were involved with."

Dorry's eyes grew sad. "You're wrong. I loved Francie dearly—but as a daughter. A daughter, not a lover."

Indignation grew in Marya. "Then how could you allow her name to be sullied by that accusation?"

Dorry took a deep swallow of whiskey this time and turned away. "I know," she whispered. "I know."

Sympathy replaced Marya's indignation. She could not look at Dorry. Unsettled, she fetched her own drink from the coffee table, forced her eyes to roam the room.

"Tell me," she said, eyes still avoiding her. "What brought all this about? Won't you tell me the whole story? Please?"

Silence fell. High tide brushed insistently against the house's foundation. It was as if Dorry and she were on a ship together adrift in a sea no one knew existed—a ship of intimate sharing, of the passing of secrets, shameful or otherwise, on which she could tell Dorry everything and Dorry would tell her whatever she asked of her. This realization proved both alarming and somehow gratifying. She, who had always held a part of herself back, protecting some self-perceived sanctum of mystery, stood defenseless before this woman.

Why her? As was her wont, Marya analyzed the revelation.

Was it her seniority—the fact Dorry was a full two decades older than Marya? Or was it the cloak of defensiveness that Dorry also had wrapped about herself? The vulnerability within the steel of her defenses matched Marya's; they were two of a kind. This gave her an odd feeling of security, a type of freedom. That, or…she had fallen in love with Dorry.

She returned her drink to the table and quickly reclaimed a seat on the sofa. She wasn't sure her shaky knees could handle this latest wave of epiphany.

"It was all so tacky," Dorry began, her gaze taking in the wide expanse of sea outside the glass doors. "Nicky and I had been friends forever. He met Isabel while working there just outside Paris and they had Francie almost immediately. We kept in touch with letters and he kept inviting me to come over. Then about ten years ago, I was in a place where I could plan a short trip to Europe and arranged to meet them."

"Where?"

"In Germany. They were on the Rhine in a little village called Lebenstraum. Isabel's parents had a ramshackle estate there. Of course, Nicky insisted I stay with them. It was all fine at first in the hubbub of arrival."

She paused to drink. "But within a week Isabel and I knew we were in trouble."

"How do you mean?"

Dorry looked at her pointedly. "Chemistry."

"Ah." Marya relaxed back into the cushions. Chemistry. "So what did you do?"

"What's the old saying? Beat feet? I backpedaled as much as possible. We kept very busy, sightseeing and going here, there and yonder. It was fun, but I was like a lovesick puppy, making a fool of myself every minute."

She laughed and shook her head at the memory.

Marya couldn't imagine Dorry making a fool of herself, but then she was beginning to realize she had no clue about the real Dorry. Ice clinking in her glass was the only sound for a long minute.

"Then one night when Nicholas and Little Bit had gone to one of her endless ballet classes, Isabel and I found ourselves in the house alone. We made light of it at first, but the chemistry grew and then she was in my arms and..." The memory seemed to stab into Dorry. Marya watched her face change into angles of grief, then resume its normal placid facade.

"We soared after that. Life was good even though we were sneaking around behind her family's back. We were in love and that was that."

"Didn't you need to come home?" Marya was rocking to and fro at the waist, the recounting of those passionate feelings hurting her. She *did* love Dorry. She knew it then.

"Sure, and that was when it became insane. I couldn't bring myself to leave her. Then Nicky mused that he wished Little Bit, who was fifteen at that time, could have had an American education and together we all hit upon the idea she was to come back with me and spend a few years here. I agreed because of the maternal way I felt toward Francie and because I knew it would keep Isabel in my life."

"And it did."

Dorry paused. "We had a little over a year together...she visited Francie often. Francie knew about our affair, I think, but she loved us both and didn't care. She would have had to be deaf and blind not to see our joy and our affection. Then she got sick."

"What happened?"

Dorry took a seat in a forest green Queen Anne chair next to the bar. She sat slumped with legs spread apart as if for support.

"She got sick," she repeated dully. "At first I—we—thought she was just not happy here, and I began making plans for her to return to Europe to her parents. But I knew something just wasn't right. She ran persistent fevers and looked…she looked gray, sickly. Isabel came in and we took her to the doctor."

"The hospital?"

"No, just Doc Hastings, here in town. He ran tests and sent us on to a specialist in Myrtle. And she never got better."

"So why did everything fall apart? How did the newspapers get involved? How did...?"

Dorry sighed and sat up straighter in her chair. Gulls called outside, the sound mournful.

"Isabel and I were stupid. We always slept together when she was here and we especially needed one another during that time for comfort. Nicky seldom came here because he was so tied up in his business. When he did he always phoned first. He didn't one time while Little Bit was under treatment and he'd been over to the hospital. He found us sleeping like two peas in a pod. Naked."

"Oh, my God," Marya murmured.

Dorry nodded agreement. "It seemed as though the earth had cracked wide open. Isabel's new pain terrified me, alienated me, and I realized how stupid I'd been to let myself get involved with her. Now all four lives were destroyed."

"And that's why he brought the charges against you?"

"Mmhmm, that's why." She lifted her drink, found it empty and absently held it in her lap.

"But it doesn't make sense. Why would he accuse you and Francie of being together when it was actually you and Isabel?"

"I wondered that at the time. I found out later that he hadn't said anything at all about her lifestyle and about Isabel and me. That came from someone else, an 'anonymous tip' delivered to Ed at the paper. I've always wondered who hated me enough to betray me that way."

She paused and watched Marya. "I've thought it was Isabel, as a way of assuaging her own guilt. At times I've thought it was Ed, just voicing something he suspected. I don't think Nicky would have said that about his daughter. Not like that."

"Why didn't you say something? Defend Francie?"

Dorry's smile tugged at Marya's heart. "Why? Why feed the monster? Little Bit was gone; papers were selling like mad. I couldn't care about anything at that point."

Marya understood how it must have been during that time and compassion welled in her. She wanted to touch Dorry, smooth her arm and let her know it would be all right. She could only sit there, a stone trapped full of swirling emotion.

"So, that's my story. If you want to write it, go ahead. The old ghosts won't stir and media sensations are even more short-lived now than they were then. I don't much care."

They sat then in a rocky but amicable peace and watched the candles that flickered around them. The house of sadness lent quiet to the night, Marya savored it before returning to the world of reality pressing in from outside. She reached into her pocket and drew forth the bracelet she'd found in the bedroom of the cottage. She rose and moved next to Dorry's chair.

"This was in my bedroom. Did you leave it there?"

Dorry squinted at the bracelet, setting aside her empty glass so she could take it from Marya. "My God, I haven't worn that since college," she muttered. "Where'd you get it?"

"I told you, from the bedroom, at the cottage. It was left in my bed."

Dorry looked up at Marya, eyes darkened by shadow. She reached out one hand and rested it against Marya's denim-clad flank. The heat of her palm sent electric lacings throughout Marya's body. She stiffened. Dorry continued to stroke her outer thigh, moving her palm slowly up and down. If she didn't stop, Marya was going to swoon.

"I didn't leave it there, Marya. And you need to go now."

Dorry took her hand away from Marya's leg and lifted it to her mouth as if quietly scolding it for its presumptuousness.

Marya walked to the door, moving through a thick jelly of desire. She wanted to get away as badly as she wanted to press her body against Dorry's. She needed to figure out what was going on, to ponder these feelings. Never before had she felt them this powerfully.

Marya closed the door behind her and, buffeted by sea wind, made her way across the sand. Once home, she stripped to T-shirt and panties and sprawled across the bed. She regretted returning the bracelet, no longer able to fondle it in lieu of Dorry as she drifted toward sleep. What had driven Dorry to touch her? Did she too feel the attraction?

She lay still, listening to the ocean noises—the clank of a buoy bell at the end of the cove, the sound of the wind tickling the treetops into dance, the knock of her hanging flowerpots as they swept the porch uprights—willing them to lull her to sleep. As she did, a new sound registered, the cautious creak of a step on sand. It was repeated, making slow, careful progress toward the house. Her heart leapt in her chest. Who was out there?

She rose and made her way to the bedroom doorway. She had drawn the curtains earlier so she could not see beyond the windows. She could no longer hear the footsteps either; her heart was beating too loudly to make them out. Cursing roundly to herself, she used every technique she had learned from the martial art, calming herself until she could hear the stealthy footsteps again. She started when the porch step creaked under someone's weight.

Whoever it was seemed to be intent on coming in for a visit.

Scanning the room for a weapon, Marya settled upon a heavy wooden candlestick. Plucking it from the kitchen table, she hoisted it high. She waited a long beat but nothing happened. Had he gone away? She moved toward the door, still wielding the candlestick, swallowed her heart and flung the door wide.

CHAPTER TWENTY-SEVEN

I hated Lucy. I hated the way she teased me. She said I could hope all day to be pretty like her but that it would never happen. She said I was ugly and smelled bad and that no one would ever want me.

"What are you doing?" Mama asked as she poked her head around my bedroom door.

"Studying," I told her, holding up the oversized blue manual as if in proof.

"You should do well," she said with a nod of her head. Her hair was wrapped around a dozen curlers, and she had on her glasses so I knew she'd been reading even though I'd heard the television droning earlier. "I'm off to bed. Work tomorrow."

"Goodnight, Mama. Sleep well," I said dutifully.

She studied me with her dark, weighing eyes. "Don't stay up too late, hear?"

"Okay, I won't."

Her thoughtful gazes had been making me uncomfortable lately. It's like she was weighing possibilities. Was it about me? Whether or not she should continue to let me live here with her? It had worked well all these years. It's not like she could abandon me in the woods again. The way she had done when I was little.

She closed my door, and I heard the squeal of her bedroom door as she closed it as well.

"Don't stay up too late," I mimicked, then grinned. I knew what I was going to do. I was gonna be up very, very late.

After a couple of infuriatingly long hours had passed, I raised my window and slid through it one leg at a time, taking it slow so that I made no sound at all. I left the window open for later and crept along the wall, away from Mama's bedroom. She was a light sleeper so I had to be careful.

Once out on the road, I was able to get some speed up, veering off to the left after about a quarter mile of fast walking. I knew this shortcut well.

Before, when I still liked Lucy, I had gone over there almost every day after school, plus lots of Saturdays. Most of the time when I was getting there she was just getting up from a long night at the lounge. Mama never cared if I went there as long as I was home for dinner and never said anything about her and who she is. Not that Lucy would have cared.

I did have to make up a big lie about who my daddy was because Lucy asked about that a lot in the beginning. Guess she wanted to see if she'd slept with him yet. I said he was an astronaut down at Cape Canaveral. That way I could just say my mama was a stay-at-home wife, another lie but it was one that had shut that nosy Lucy up.

Nosy Lucy. I was tired of her nosing in my life and then using what she found out to say rude things to me just to hurt my feelings.

Lucy's house loomed in the darkness. Luckily she had no dogs. The Grisham family's hound two blocks over set in to baying, though. I guess he heard me even though I was trying to be as quiet as possible. It was also lucky that Lucy's place was on a large lot with no neighbors close by who would see me.

Lucy was probably drunk anyway and wouldn't even hear me come into the house. I just hoped she didn't have a man with her. I knew she often picked up losers from Smithy's lounge then brought them home for sex. I'd done it once or twice myself which is how I met Lucy all those years ago.

I crept to the dark side of the house where I'd be hidden from the streetlights on Lawson Avenue. I slowly, patiently rounded the two dark sides feeling each window. Just as I began to fear I'd have to break one, my hand found a screen that was loose over an open window.

Carefully, ever so slowly, I used my fingers as soft pry bars to pull the screen from its frame. I lowered it to the ground and listened at the window. There was no sound. I closed my eyes, trying to remember which room this window let into. After a minute or two it came to me. It was the bathroom. This window was over the bathtub.

Feeling a bit more confident that I wouldn't be heard from the bedroom, I raised the window and lifted myself onto the wooden sill. I swung one leg over and levered my body over and into the bathtub. A plastic bottle fell with a muffled thud and rolled to and fro in the bottom of the tub. I waited for it to still before I moved again. All was still silent in the house, and I made no sound as I stepped from the tub and onto the pocked linoleum floor. I was worried about floor creaks so I stepped carefully into the hallway. I turned right and made my way into the bedroom.

I could see that she was asleep by the glow of the night-light. She looked almost angelic lying there. I crept close and pushed my shoes off, then lifted the sheet and slid into the bed next to her. She didn't move.

I listened to her gentle snoring for a moment. Power filled me. She didn't know I was there. I was in complete control of the situation.

I turned to face her and caught the faint tang of alcohol on her breath. A man had been there recently; I could smell him on the sheets and on her.

How should I wake her?

She was wearing a sheer, very short nightgown. I touched its nylon softness, rubbing the fabric between my fingertips. One spaghetti strap had fallen to the side as she sprawled on her back and the rounded side of one breast gleamed in the dimness. I laid my palm against it, gently, softly. The sleepy warmth of her seeped into me, empowering me further. I teased one finger against the fabric covering that nipple. To my delight, it hardened beneath my touch.

Lucy moaned and stirred so I stilled until she fell into slumber again. I smiled. I was not ugly. I was beautiful, just as beautiful as Lucy. And I could make her body respond to me. I slid my palm along her belly until I reached the end of the short nightgown. My hand found fur and dampness. I laughed silently. Yes, a man had been there.

"Who was he?" I whispered. "Was it Roy? He's always had the hots for you."

She didn't answer, but I could sense her struggling toward wakefulness. I pressed my fingers against the fur and moved them, applying pressure. She moaned and turned toward me, a sleepy smile on her lips. I pressed my mouth to hers. She responded at first, wrapping one arm around my neck, keeping her eyes closed. At some point she must have sensed my difference for she began to push away. I held her as I laughed quietly.

"No," she said. "No, I don't want that."

I pressed my fingers upward and they entered her easily.

"Yes, yes, you do," I said, even as I pushed harder.

CHAPTER TWENTY-EIGHT

Dorry stood on the porch, gazing into the trees where Denton's body had been found. When Marya's door flew wide, she turned and looked at her, eyes filled with pain.

Marya suffered an onslaught of emotions then. Would Dorry hurt her? Was she the killer? She held the candlestick high, wondering if she could defend herself against the master. She was so powerful, so well trained. Did Marya stand a chance?

Dorry looked at the candlestick and dropped her head to her chest, shaking it in disbelief. "I've never killed anyone, Marya. Never intend to, if I can help it. You, of all people, should know what I'm about, should feel it in your bones."

Marya studied Dorry and trusted her own inner knowledge. She dropped the candleholder to the floor, and it rolled noisily toward the table as if going home.

"Dorry, I..."

Dorry came toward her and Marya was in her arms. Dorry held her a long time, then pulled back so she could see her eyes.

"Chemistry?" she asked, her gaze both tender and compelling.

"Chemistry," Marya answered.

Their first kiss would never leave her. Dorry's lips branded Marya hers as surely as any commitment ceremony would ever do. Marya found herself pulled into her, her goodness and sweetness, and the coldness of their past relationship evaporated into so much ocean spray.

Marya pulled back to study Dorry with amazement. Perhaps, as the poet Keats had so aptly put it, there was richest juice in this poison flower. Dorry kissed her again and they were inside the cottage, door closed to the night outside. The kiss lasted another lingering eternity and she found herself transported. Dorry's sinuous lips and tongue nibbled at Marya's, possessing, releasing, possessing, releasing in a sensual ebb and flow.

Her body began to ache, her limbs grew heavy and sluggish as they swelled with the blood of desire.

Dorry's lips left hers, breath moist and fragrant across Marya's skin. They followed a languorous sampling course, tasting her cheeks, her throat, her ear—knowing just the right feather touch whisper Marya needed there—before conquering Marya's lips again. The sudden possession caused a deep throbbing—a persistent drumbeat—in the center of her being. Moisture welled and her thighs dampened as she pressed them together.

"Oh, Dorry, what's happening?" she asked in a murmur. She'd never experienced such arousal.

"What is it, what's wrong?" Dorry searched her face with a worried gaze.

"I feel...here," Marya let one hand slide across her lower belly.

"You feel what? Desire? Need? Do you want me?"

"Oh yes, all of that," she answered.

"Then have me, baby. Don't be afraid. I'm yours." Passion trembled in Dorry's voice.

Their eyes met in the dimness, Dorry's deepening with that ardent energy Marya was becoming so familiar with, and she leapt to return Dorry's insistent kisses. Prompted by the fire in her body, she slid her hands along Dorry's solid waist and up to her breasts. Allowed at last to heft their marvelous weight and softness, she was delirious with gratitude. She closed her eyes, focusing on the sensation.

Dorry touched her, under her shirt, hot palms trailing a fiery essence along her skin. Breath hitched in Dorry's throat and she trembled as her hands reached higher, finding Marya's nipples erect and needy. Marya lifted apologetic eyes but found Dorry's gaze steady into hers, demanding. She quaked inside as the lightning in those eyes roused an ionic storm within her. She began to change subtly, her own need rising and taking her over as Dorry's hands caressed her skin. Dorry *knew* her, knew what she needed, what she wanted. She could read her. Marya had realized, at last, the intricate intimacy she had been craving from a lover. It was here, in Dorry's full understanding of her need.

CHAPTER TWENTY-NINE

Her body entwined with the strong one next to her, Marya listened to the gentle pull of Dorry's breath. It matched the ocean sighing outside. Dorry's face was lovely in sleep—more serene than she'd ever seen it. The pale blue sheet draped across her like sky across clouds. Marya reached to run one fingertip across a crease pulled taut across one breast.

"That feels nice," Dorry said, startling Marya.

"You're awake," Marya told her unnecessarily.

Eyes of cornflower blue found and studied her, searching for signs of damage or regret, Marya supposed, or perhaps acceptance. She smiled to show Dorry the way it was.

Dorry pressed heated lips to Marya's forehead.

"Dorry, last night...I can't begin to tell you..."

"The sex is good and this thing between us is even better."

Marya blushed at the candor. "Well, for me, yes."

Dorry smiled and Marya could see a delicious sense of contentment in her. "And me, as well. I am totally smitten with you and that's that. I tried not to fall head over heels because I like my life simple and this is complicated."

Marya mused over the words, realizing she understood what Dorry meant. Relationships implied complication. Two instead of one. Endless compromise and adjustment. But wasn't that what she had been seeking?

"I can't pinpoint what it is that draws me to you," Marya said finally. "It seems I wait for the days I'll see you, whether at class or the way you keep popping up in my life. At first I was annoyed, but now I'm eager for any glimpse of you. Being in your bed is like prayer."

Dorry watched Marya with some confusion. "Prayer?" she teased with a grin and drew her finger along Marya's jawline. "Are you getting religious on me?"

"All my life I've been looking for this touch. The intimacy is so powerful." Marya's eyes found hers.

"How does it make you feel?"

"Embarrassed when our eyes meet like this, because I know you see the depth of my passion."

"And the intricacies of what pleases you," Dorry added, causing Marya to flame in acute embarrassment. She remembered the arousal she had felt in Dorry's arms, the insanity of her desire.

"Yes. I can be honest with you. I can reveal myself." She rolled onto her stomach and looked across at Dorry. "My question is why? Why is it so much easier with you?"

It was hard to believe Dorry's eyes had ever seemed cold to her. They were fond, even tender, as she pondered the question. "Have you ever been in a relationship with an older woman, one, say, twenty years older?"

"No. What does that have to do with anything?"

"Maybe it's maternal. It's often said the best thing about a lesbian partner is that she's not just your lover but your mother and sister as well. Have we come so far in so little time that we can be all that to one another?"

Marya snorted with laughter. "Oh right, I can see you as my mother."

Dorry chuckled thoughtfully. "I do feel motherly toward you—even though you're such a newshound. As for you, perhaps being with an older woman implies safety and security and you can relax—be more yourself."

Marya rested an arm along the firm expanse of Dorry's abdomen.

"Maybe," Marya mused quietly, "but I certainly don't feel childlike in your arms. Just the opposite." She pressed her mouth to Dorry's and whispered, "You make me insatiable."

Dorry placed her strong hand over Marya's and guided it to where she wanted it. Their gazes found one another and locked as they became one. Dorry moaned and arched her body into Marya's.

***

When Marya arrived at The Way of Hand and Foot *dojang* later that day, Dorry had closed for the day and left. Rob was waiting for her outside, sitting on the sidewalk next to the side door. He had earbuds in his ears and was joyfully bebopping to music only he could hear. She pulled the Trooper into a parking slot next to the side door. He noticed her and stood. He was still in street clothes, his uniform in the duffel he carried. He pulled out his earbuds as she grabbed her own bag from the car and locked its doors.

"Hey, Rob, how have you been?" Marya asked as she unlocked the *dojang's* side entrance. "Any more bullying?"

He shrugged. "No, not this week. I've been avoiding him though."

"Good idea. So, what? You work with this guy?"

"Yeah." Rob followed her into the *dojang*. "We're both mail handlers for Conners Electric. He likes to show off, prove that he's a badass to all the other guys in the break room. So he picks fights or throws heavy crap at me. Stuff like that."

"Wow, that sucks," Marya said as she flicked on the overhead lights in the mat area. "The moves you'll learn here will help defuse any situation like that."

"Is it hard to learn? *Hapkido*, I mean?"

Marya studied him as they stood next to the changing rooms. "I won't lie and say it's easy or something you can learn overnight," she said. "Anything good takes true dedication."

Rob nodded. "I know. That's what my mama says all the time."

Marya smiled and laid one hand on the changing room door. "Smart woman. Well, let's get changed and I'll see you on the mats."

The session went well. Rob was a good, focused student and quickly learned the basic grapple holds and a few takedowns. Marya stressed to him the importance of knowing when to stop applying bone-breaking pressure. She was satisfied that he understood the danger.

"You only respond this way when an opponent lunges for you. Anything else and you break the unwritten code of *hapkido*. This discipline is not for offense. It's defense only."

"Yes, ma'am," Rob said. He was panting and sweating heavily. After two hours of intense work, they were both exhausted.

"Okay, let's call it a night, what do you say?" Marya asked as she patted him on the shoulder. "I don't know about you, but I bet I'm going to have a sore muscle or two tomorrow."

Rob laughed and nodded. "Yeah, I think we both will. Thanks a lot for working with me like this. I feel much better already about dealing with that jerk at work."

In the changing room, Marya's thoughts turned to Dorry and the late supper they had planned for that evening. She was able to release the excitement she'd held at bay all during her class with Rob. Rushing through a shower and donning clothing, she emerged back into the *dojang* in record time. Even so, Rob was waiting for her.

"So, are we ready?" she asked, checking both changing room doors to make sure they were secure. She switched off the first rank of *dojang* lights, then the second as the two of them progressed toward the foyer area just inside the side entrance.

"You didn't go into the front lobby, did you?" she asked as she paused by the door. She glanced toward the sets of wide doors that led to the front.

Rob shook his head as he inserted one earbud. "Nope, I was with you almost the whole time."

Marya nodded and ushered him out and pulled the door tight. She realized that her car was the only one in the deserted lot. "Hey, where's your car?"

"In the shop again," he said with a heavy sigh. "Bum transmission. It's always going out on me."

"I had one like that once," Marya said as she slid into the driver's seat. "Hop in. I'll give you a ride home."

"Better not. My mama's coming to get me. She's just down the street at her bridge club. I told her it would be about two hours so she should be here in a few minutes. Her old biddy card friends get tired out after more than a couple hours anyway." He grinned at her, coaxing a return smile from Marya. "Thank you for the offer, though."

"Well, okay. If you're sure," Marya said slowly. She hesitated. "Are you sure?"

He laughed. "I'm a big boy. You don't have to worry about me."

Marya laughed at herself. "I know…I'm an old softie. You tell anyone I went all maternal and I'll be the one beating up on your ass." She pulled the door closed.

She backed out and he waved once before sliding down to sit against the wall on the sidewalk that surrounded the building. He was fiddling with his music player. Several outside lights had sputtered into life in the dusk and they made a halo surrounding him as he sat there.

"Let it go, Marya," she told herself as she pulled onto the two-lane road that ran in front of the business. She couldn't shake a dire feeling and hoped he'd be safe there all alone. Her thoughts flew then to the lover who waited for her. Suddenly she was eager to get home. Rob was right. He was a big boy.

About a quarter of a mile down the road, Marya was forced to stand on her brake as an oncoming vehicle inexplicably veered over into her lane. There was a moment of worry that the car wouldn't right itself, but it did and as it passed, Marya peered at the driver's window. She reared back and suffered a moment of shock. She knew that face, that hair.

Turning into the parking lot of the Tecumseh Baptist Church, Marya executed a U-turn and rolled the car along until she reached the parking lot of The Way of Hand and Foot. She passed by slowly, watching as Rob climbed into the passenger side of the car that had passed her. A car that she now recognized as belonging to Emily Davies, the business manager of the *Schuyler Times*. Emily was Rob Tyler's mother? She never would have guessed.

CHAPTER THIRTY

Work the next morning passed by in a blur. Marya went through the motions, acting and reacting almost mechanically, all her thoughts fixed on Dorry and the passionate night they had spent together.

Before they parted that morning, they made plans for a late dinner together at her house after their work days were over. Marya was glad they were going to be together again soon. There was an emptiness, almost an ache, where their bodies had pressed against one another.

"You know, they never did get along." Dallas's voice sounded next to her ear.

"Who's that?" Marya asked, swiveling around in her chair so she could see the social columnist.

"Him and Dorry," she replied, pointing to the computer screen. Marya had opened the Barnes Taekwondo page on her computer to get the phone number.

"Fred Barnes?"

"Yep, he always had this sort of superior attitude that really got him in a lot of trouble. Of course, Dorry thinks she's something special too, due to her family being so old and established here in Schuyler Point and all. They mixed like oil and water."

"I knew there had to be water under that bridge," she replied, trying not to let Dallas's attitude about Dorry get to her. "He acted very strange when I mentioned Dorry's name to him."

"I reckon," Dallas said with a smirk. "She mopped up the floor with him at a national competition once. He hasn't been the same since."

They both turned as one when Dallas's phone let out a staccato peal.

"I guess that's me," she said, hurrying off.

Marya turned back to her computer and called the number for the Barnes *dojang*. Though she heard it ring numerous times, no one answered and she was shunted over to voice mail. She left a message, asking Barnes to call her as soon as possible. She had realized after coming in that morning and beginning work on the fund-raising piece that she was missing several pieces of crucial information, such as the names of the participants in the taekwondo exercises. Writing around the information she was lacking for the moment, she worked on the article for the next half hour. Then she called the Barnes *dojang* again. Getting voice mail once more, she left another message, this time stressing the urgency of her situation. Forty minutes later there was still no response, and the fund-raising piece was finished except for the names she was missing.

She rose and strode into Emily's office.

"Hey, Emily, were you at the fund-raiser Saturday?"

Emily looked at her with wide, stunned eyes. "No, no, why would I go there?"

Marya almost said something about Rob and Emily watching him and his class display their skills but something, some hunch, stayed her voice. "Just needed some names for a story I'm working on," she said instead.

Emily leaned forward across her desk, suddenly all smiles and helpfulness, as her plump, ringed hands caressed a pencil. "Oh, get Dallas to help you with that. I think she was there and she knows just about everybody in these parts. I'm sure she'll be glad to help you out."

Marya smiled and turned to go. "Good idea," she said, her mind whirling with possibilities. Was Emily hiding Rob? There were no photos of him in the office, and in all the time Marya had been with the *Schuyler Times*, no one had ever mentioned her having a son.

Outside Emily's office Marya stared at a mostly empty office. Dallas had disappeared. Ed and Marvin, she remembered, were at a PTO meeting at the elementary school. She heard music from the back but knew the pasteup guys would be of little help.

She sat at her desk and made sure the article she'd been slaving on all morning was saved to a thumb drive. She stuck the drive in her bag, grabbed up the bag from the desk, and headed to the front desk.

"Going out to the Barnes *dojang*," she told Carol. Pausing abruptly, she turned back and studied the receptionist. "Are you *ever* going to have that baby?" she asked.

Carol took a deep breath and studied Marya with equanimity. "Nope. I don't think so. I think she's in there for good. Buddy says we should start charging her rent because she's been making me eat so much."

Marya laughed as she left the building, letting the door slide closed behind her.

***

Marya easily found her way back to Barnes Taekwondo. She was pleased to see the business was open; she had been afraid it was closed for some reason, but there were a number of cars in the small parking area in front. She parked near the main door and, snatching up her notebook, went inside.

The front lobby was deserted. She waited a few minutes, striding over to the wall of trophies on the north wall. She was dismayed to find them dusty and neglected.

"Such a shame," she muttered. If they were going to use trophies to define their sport, the least they could do is to take care of them.

After another five minutes of waiting, Marya opened the door to the *dojang* and peeked inside. A belt she didn't recognize was leading a small class. Barnes was in the back, watching instead of teaching. He was reclining in a folding chair, one hand to his chin, watching the class as they went through their *poomses*.

Marya removed her shoes, then slipped inside and stepped over to Barnes. She tapped his shoulder and he looked up at her as if awakening from a deep sleep.

"Hey, Mr. Barnes. Remember me? Marya Brock from the *Times*?"

She waited until he nodded his head before continuing in a low whisper. "I'm working on the fund-raising story and I never got the names from you—the names of the students who were sharing the art that day."

Barnes rattled off three names, and Marya scribbled them into her notebook. He watched her and silence grew between them.

"You're that dyke's student, aren't you?" he asked suddenly.

Marya recoiled. "I beg your pardon?"

"Dorcas. The town lesbian." His voice became a high contralto as he mentioned the name of her business in a mocking tone. "The Way of Hand and Foot."

Marya's mouth fell open.

"I could think of some other names for it. Because of what she does. You know, in the bedroom." He said this in a low, suggestive voice.

Marya was overcome with such fury that she wasn't sure she could speak. Strange angry gurgles issued from her mouth.

"I bet you're one too. You kinda look like one, but you carry that mild-mannered reporter air so no one can really tell." He sat back in his chair and eyed her speculatively.

Marya had been angry many times in her life but never infuriated to the point of being unable to speak, much less respond to his rude, offensive ramblings.

He continued in a thoughtful mien. "I wonder what she's been teaching you over at that joke of a school."

He rose and moved toward Marya, who still stood, stunned into inaction. Without warning, he slapped her cheek lightly but with enough force to hurt. "What will you do about that, huh? You got any moves?"

Marya's eyes filled with tears from the stinging pain. She was aware that the students had stopped working out and were watching the bizarre scene playing out between the two of them. She spoke then, putting aside the fury seething inside her. "*Master* Barnes, I think this has gone far enough."

She stressed his title, reminding him of the standards by which he should be living.

He grinned wolfishly. "What? You got nothing? Come on, baby dyke, show me what you got."

He spun and shot out one leg toward Marya's side but she quickly, automatically, blocked it, her body crouching low, arms outstretched in protective stance.

Barnes danced like a boxer, legs spread and fists raised at chest level. Marya watched him cautiously, her fury shoved aside by the cool head she needed to fight an opponent. They circled one another and then Barnes lifted his left leg in a side kick to her abdomen. She blocked it effectively, but he spun like a top and rammed the heel of the other leg into her side. Pain exploded through her body and stars danced in front of her eyes. All breath was expelled from her body, and she realized that she could not inhale and draw new air into her lungs. She stumbled backward and bent forward, her eyes never leaving Barnes. After what seemed like hours but indeed was only seconds, she was able to inhale and the grayness in her vision cleared. And he was coming for her again, that carnivorous grin splitting his unshaven face.

"I don't think so," she gasped out and, ignoring the pain blazing through her like an electric current, she relaxed every muscle in her body and swept Barnes away from her as he charged. She panted, one hand seeking to comfort her side as he rose from the floor. His belt, a young man less than twenty years old, moved to help him up and dissuade him from further attack. Barnes shoved him so hard he went sprawling across the bare floor.

Marya, though she appeared unaffected and relaxed, was ready for him should he renew his advance. Her mind went through the best takedown from her *hapkido* training. *Take out a man's knees and he cannot fight* kept rolling through her brain. A part of her didn't want to harm the master but obviously he had become a mad dog. He needed to be put down in some way and quickly.

Her mind was made up in a fraction of a second. As Barnes charged again, she grasped his neck, right over the carotid artery, and used the weight of her body and a leg sweep to take him to the floor. She focused all her weight on her arms and hands and though his legs and hips thrashed below her, she kept a steady pressure on his carotid. Several minutes later, he was unconscious. Marya rolled off him, falling supine to the floor. Every expansion of her chest as she gasped for air felt like a knife stab to her ribs. One rib was likely fractured, possibly more.

The belt hovered over her, eyes searching her face. "Oh, ma'am, are you okay? I don't know what that was about. I've...I've never seen him do anything like that before."

Marya nodded to show she'd heard him, but she wasn't up for speaking at that moment.

The young man helped her to her feet and retrieved her notebook and pen, pressing them into her hands. Marya glanced around once and saw the adolescent students huddled into protective groups, eyes wide as they watched her.

"Y'all all need to go home now," she gasped. Her gaze flew to the belt. "Can you get them out of here? Get them home?" She wrapped one arm protectively around her abdomen.

"Yes, ma'am. Yes. What will you do?"

Marya knew he was worried that she would press charges against his master. "I don't know," she whispered as she staggered toward the door. "I don't know."

Pressing charges against Barnes might just exacerbate the situation she was currently in with the local police force. She didn't need witnesses relating what Barnes had said to her before he attacked. Not to mention the grief it would bring to her parents if she—and her lifestyle—became the latest news of the week. Then again, maybe Barnes's violent actions would lead police to investigate him for Denton's murder. She paused, one hand on the closed door. No, she couldn't chance it.

Outside the day had turned muggy. Marya limped to her car and painfully lifted herself into the seat. She switched on the engine and turned the air-conditioning on full blast. Sweat evaporated from her forehead and cheeks as she levered the car into gear and headed to the hospital she'd seen out on Route 17. Her shocked mind could only gape at the idea that Fred Barnes had attacked her for no apparent reason.

***

Leaving the hospital several hours later with her cracked ribs taped securely, Marya decided to head back to the office. She needed to finish the fund-raiser article so she would make deadline. She also wanted to learn more about the man who'd attacked her. Maybe the fight had been a good thing, just the impetus she needed to investigate further concerning who might have the best reason to kill Denton. Barnes had just proven that he was crazy enough to harm someone. Was he the one who murdered Denton? She touched her bandaged ribs as she pulled out on the highway. He was strong enough.

No matter how hard she wracked her brain, unfortunately, Marya could come up with no good reason for anyone wanting Denton out of the way. The man was the most inoffensive person Marya had ever met. Could all this have come about because of the 1996 purse-snatching incident?

She frowned at the highway. Not likely. It was just that there was nothing else to suggest that Denton's actions, rash or otherwise, could have contributed in any way to his death. Following that logic, she had to assume his murder was a random criminal act. This assumption made everything a bit more difficult. Most murders were committed by someone the victim was close to, making it much easier to ferret out the perpetrator. A random murder, on the other hand, would be much more difficult to solve. The murderer could be anyone, even, as Ed surmised, someone long gone from Marstown.

She knew from Dallas and Dorry that Fred Barnes had been part of their local group of friends. This made him a more desirable suspect in her eyes.

Oddly enough, the *Schuyler Times* office was still almost deserted. She saw only Ed who waved at her from behind his computer.

"The B-front will be shooting toward you in a minute or two," she called to him as she carefully sat at her desk. The painkillers had kicked in, but any lateral movement hurt like hell. She fished out her notebook and thumb drive from her bag, popped the thumb drive into the computer, added the missing names, gave the article one more cursory glance, then sent it over to Ed. She inhaled a deep but careful sigh and typed Fred Barnes into the search engine. Opening his business website, she spent some time looking for craziness. Nothing. She was frustrated. She sighed and sat back in her squeaky office chair.

It was all too easy to imagine Sheriff Gennis and his pet deputy Thomas driving up to the cottage with a warrant for her arrest. Or worse, one for Dorry's arrest. If that happened, they would never be able to prove their innocence.

Chewing a thumbnail, she let her fingers roam across the keyboard. After a moment of hesitation, afraid of what she might find, she opened a new database and typed in the name Frederick Barnes. She held her breath as she waited, one hand absently soothing her ribs.

She was rewarded with a red star. Pay dirt. Intrigued, she leaned forward and moved the cursor to the details button. She clicked it and began avidly reviewing the facts it revealed.

In 2004, a restraining order had been issued to keep Frederick Barnes away from none other than Dorcas Wood. Her mouth fell open. She had sensed there was some bad history there, but nothing quite like that.

She read on, curiosity gnawing at her. The restraining order had been issued twice, she saw. It looked like old Barnes had been stalking Dorry. The original police report cited trespassing, harassing phone calls in the night, slander and even libel. Since the second order had been issued, he was now not allowed to come within one hundred feet of Dorry and could not enter the premises of her land or business without her express permission submitted and approved through law enforcement channels. Wow.

Marya wondered why Barnes had been stalking Dorry. Love? Hatred? It could be either. Maybe because of the Francie publicity? Or was there something else?

She sat back and remembered how Barnes had looked while attacking her. Should she go ahead and report the attack to the police? She'd been too shocked to decide before but he *could* be the one who killed Denton, and due to his past, he would be a person of interest to the Coburn County police.

She sighed. Her head was fuzzy from the pain meds. She decided she would talk to Dorry that evening, and they would make their first decision as a couple.

CHAPTER THIRTY-ONE

There was something wrong. Dorry knew it as soon as she stepped up to the back entrance after rounding the building. Something just didn't feel right. The nape of her neck began to tingle and her heart began to thud.

Then she saw it.

Two years ago, a little girl named Polly Reynolds had taken classes under Dorry. She made it all the way to purple belt before her abusive, backward father had prevailed over her mother and pulled her out of the school. During her time there, Polly had drawn numerous pictures of Dorry and the other teachers and students. They were wonderful depictions of the *dojang* and staff, so Dorry had kept many of them tacked to the walls of her office. She had looked at them often while pondering what life might have been like for little Polly if she'd had different parents.

Now, at her feet, lay a portion of one of those familiar drawings. It was a lower left corner of a drawing of the interior of the *dojang*.

Slowly, disbelievingly, Dorry reached out and lifted the scrap of artwork. The torn edge was jagged and crumpled as if ripped with great force.

A sudden sick feeling bloomed in her stomach. She pushed at the unlocked door, swinging it open. Still not completely comprehending what she was seeing, her mind shocked into numbness, Dorry stepped inside.

"My God," she whispered. "What has happened here?"

The long hallway that led into the *dojang* was littered with shards of paper and crumpled file folders. Dorry stepped into the midst of them and peered inside her office. She gasped in despair. The room was a shambles. Mementos from her students and staff had been tossed about, some of them destroyed. Her file cabinets gaped open, their contents scattered about the room.

Stepping further in, she saw that the drawers of her desk had been pried open. Office supplies were piled in haphazard fashion on the floor behind the desk. Even her office chair had been flipped over. It was now balanced precariously against the bookshelves on the back wall. She saw to her dismay that many of her books and their covers had been ripped apart as well as being thrown helter-skelter. And, most hurtful of all, precious framed photos had been shattered against the floor and desk.

Terrified at what else she was going to find, Dorry left the office and strode down the littered hallway into the *dojang*. It too had been ransacked, pads and weights tossed carelessly hither and yon, many of the pads sliced with a knife. Even the cord holding up the heavy kick bag had been slashed. The huge black and silver bag lay on the *dojang* floor like a wounded soldier.

Dorry wasn't sure what to feel. Immense anger warred with intense pain. She stood helpless, grinding her palms together as her eyes tried to drink in all the damage that had been done to her livelihood and to her life. Her gaze fell on the banners filled with inspirational messages that she had read every day for the past decade. They too were torn; the word *excellence* hung to one side, moving listlessly in an errant breeze.

She turned and walked slowly back to her office. Noticing her cashbox lying busted open and empty next to the printer stand and feeling the need to take some action, she righted the phone and called 911.

"I need to report a…a…burglary," she said in a shocky, incredulous whisper. She had to repeat it three times before the dispatcher could hear her properly. After hanging up, she started a search for her business checkbook. Unable to find it, she started mentally listing the steps she was going to need to take to protect herself and the business from identity theft. Then she remembered that the checkbook was still in her truck. She had taken it home for balancing the day before.

"A lucky break, that," she muttered to herself.

She studied the damage again as she waited for the police to arrive and her gaze fell on the scheduling calendar she kept on the south wall next to the door. It hung crookedly now so she had to tilt her head to read the entry posted on the previous day. Her mouth fell into a grim line.

***

The *Schuyler Times* office was a madhouse that afternoon. Carol's water had broken while she was at her desk, and she had been rushed to the hospital in the first stages of labor. That had left Emily at the front desk trying to figure out how to direct and transfer the calls that were coming in while doing her own work. Adding to the hubbub were the frequent updates from Buddy as he kept Ed and the others posted on Carol's progress.

Marya was busy trying to make story determinations for the next week's issue when her cell phone rang. She saw by the caller ID that it was Dorry and a warm cloud of remembered joy suffused her.

"Hello, sweetheart," she said as she answered. "You would not even believe how crazy it is here today. I have so much to tell you. Carol is having the baby..."

There was silence on the line.

"Dorry? Are you there?"

"I should have known better than to trust you, to let you into my life," Dorry said finally, her voice low and strangled back into her throat. "I *told* you to make sure the door was locked. I *told* you how important it was."

"Dorry? What has happened? What do you mean?"

"I...I can't do this right now." The phone line went dead.

Marya stood stunned for a moment, her mind and heart racing. Something had happened at the *dojang*.

She grabbed up her bag and painfully hobbled to Ed's office. "Ed, I gotta go. I'm sorry."

Ed looked at her with bloodshot, weary eyes. "You can't leave now. Marvin is at a Supervisors' meeting and there are not enough of us here as it is."

Marya just shook her head and biting her lip, stumbled from his office and out to her car.

A trio of police cars and a rescue unit surrounded the *dojang* when Marya pulled up. Suddenly worried about Dorry's well-being, she extricated herself from the car as fast as she could and limped inside through the gaping back door.

The sight that met her gaze brought sudden tears to her eyes. The Way of Hand and Foot had been destroyed. Furniture was toppled, mirrors broken, papers and file folders scattered everywhere.

She made her way down the long hall leading from the back door, her mind reeling from this beastly, willful destruction of property. The *dojang* was in similar disarray. Dorry was perched on the end of one cabinet, law officers and rescue personnel hovering around her. She looked awful, her face ashen and drawn.

"Oh, Dorry, what happened?" Marya said as she approached.

Deputy Thomas was there. He moved back from Dorry, but he and Sheriff Gennis watched closely as Marya took Dorry's arm. "Are you okay?"

Dorry jerked her arm from Marya, causing her to hiss in sudden pain. Seeing the men's interest, Dorry grabbed Marya by the elbow and pulled her to one side, away from the others.

"How could you do this to me?" she spat. "I *trusted* you, Marya!"

"It was locked, Dorry, I swear it," Marya whispered. "I swear it."

"Then how did this happen? The door wasn't damaged. It had to be unlocked." Dorry watched her face with hurt, angry eyes.

"I…it had to be Rob," Marya said finally. "He wasn't with me the whole time. He must have gone into the front lobby and unlocked the door. The side door was locked. I'm sure of it."

"Oh, that's easy," Dorry said. "Pass the buck. You and only you were responsible for checking all the doors before you left."

"Dorry, I'm so sorry. I…I didn't want to let you down…"

Dorry glared at her. "Well, you did let me down and because I trusted you—which I know better, I *know* not to do that—but because I did…because I was weak, I've lost everything. Do you even understand what that means?"

Marya bristled. "Of course! I'm not stupid. But Dorry, we can build it back up together." She touched Dorry's arm. "Together we can do anything."

Dorry's eyes lifted and they were so cold they chilled Marya to the bone. "Together, ha! I knew better than to try and have a relationship. I never want to see you again, Marya Brock. Just stay out of my goddamned way from now on. Just leave me alone."

She strode away and Marya's heart dropped from her body. The pain of Dorry's rejection was one hundred times worse than that of her broken ribs. One hundred. She turned and hurried from the *dojang*, afraid she would start screaming out her anguish there in front of God and everyone. Ten minutes later she pulled off at a beach access beside Route 17. Sitting in her Trooper with the windows rolled up, she did scream. She screamed and cried until the pain in her ribs was almost as bad as the pain in her soul.

CHAPTER THIRTY-TWO

Struggling to come to terms with this latest bout of feeling alone and abandoned, Marya decided she needed a stiff drink. It was early in the day, but she didn't much care. Hiccupping and swiping at her eyes, she drove toward Myrtle Beach. Dorry could not, would not have such power over her.

The late afternoon was fine, the kind of day that was so fragrant and peaceful it made natives speak of soft, delicate baby hair. Marya rode along, window down, mind numb, staring dumbly at the sights. Shopkeepers still had heavily laden tables out on the sidewalks, bored employees lolling next to them counting the hours until closing. A lot of people were out and about. Pink, freshly bathed and nattily dressed tourists on their way to dinner. Waitresses scurrying along the sidewalks fiddling with their hair even as they donned their aprons and prepared to serve them.

Traffic wasn't as bad as she had expected, probably because the winter rush hadn't yet started. She was able to drive mindlessly as she pondered her losses. Would Dorry relent? Reconsider? Knowing Dorry's personality, Marya doubted it. She had seen the coldness in those eyes, the lack of forgiveness there, and remembered well Dorry's aloofness when they'd first met.

She wondered whether or not she even would have a place to sleep that night. Tears filled her eyes again, but she blinked them back. She would be damned if she'd wallow in self-pity.

Forcing thoughts of Dorry from her mind, Marya began looking for and soon found King Street. There was a gay bar there that she'd seen listed in one of the local magazines and been planning to try it out at some point. Now was as good a time as any, she figured.

The club, called Rainbow Spheres, was small and nondescript when she finally located it, but decked with hanging outside lights that no doubt made it more festive in the evening. No matter. The general tackiness of its daylight appearance better suited her current mood. She parked, gingerly climbed out of the Trooper and slowly made her way into the place.

The long bar running the length of the back was inviting, but she didn't think her sore ribs would allow her to mount a barstool with any comfort. She decided to claim a small table in a corner where she could drink and cry in dark solitude.

The trio of patrons turned and examined her as she eased her way over to it and sat down, then returned to their drinks and their conversations. Marya ignored them, staring instead at her hands, clasped tightly together on the worn wooden top of the table. She still wasn't thinking, but the numbness was wearing off, replaced by a growing anger. Anger that Dorry would so quickly assume that she was to blame. Anger that she had made no effort to hear her out or look at the facts instead of her first, shocked perceptions.

She was better off without Dorry in her life, Marya decided. Painful as this all was, it was better that it ended now. She had no tolerance for intolerance. She might be a reporter, might have to look for the right and wrong of things, the good and bad of things, but that didn't mean she was ruled by absolutes. Sometimes things were gray. Not black and white, even though one might want them to be. But gray. Gray.

"What'll you have, hon?" A waitress had appeared next to Marya's table. She was young, in her twenties, with long, dark hair drawn back in a haphazard ponytail. On her the hairstyle looked great. Her dark brown eyes looked as if they were perpetually amused, her mouth was wide and fun-loving. She regarded Marya, her head tilting to one side. "You look like something the cat dragged in. What happened to you?"

Marya shook her head. "You wouldn't believe the day I've had. I was beaten up…my ribs broken…by a crazy martial arts guy…Then my girlfriend's—my ex-girlfriend's—business was broken in to and destroyed and she broke up with me, blaming me for what happened."

"Dayum!" the waitress exclaimed. "Are you gonna be all right?"

Marya nodded. "I think so, but three fingers of scotch on the rocks might help."

"I hear you," she said. "Single malt coming up. I'm Cybil, by the way."

Marya extended her hand. "Marya Brock. Pleased to meet you, Cybil."

Cybil shook the proffered hand. "And me you, Marya. Be right back."

With concerted effort, Marya pushed Dorry from her mind. When Cybil returned with the scotch, she talked her into joining her.

"So why does your name seem familiar to me, Marya?" Cybil asked, her hands fiddling with a bar towel.

"I write for the *Schuyler Times*. That might be where you've seen it." Marya took a long pull off the tumbler of scotch and was delighted when the heat-generating liquid relaxed her clenched stomach.

"Oh yeah! That article you did last week on the woman with all those dogs...I bet that was fun. What was it like interviewing her?"

Marya chuckled and proceeded to tell Cybil about the three hours she had spent getting up close and personal with the woman's family of fourteen dogs. The woman had expected her to remember their names after the interview was over.

Sitting with Cybil, relaxing in what seemed like the first time in months, felt amazingly good. Felt a lot, in fact, like the days, back before Kim, when Marya would have worked all night on Miss Cybil and then taken her home with her to have someone to warm her body and her bed. Old habits die hard, she discovered. Before long, she was flirting shamelessly with her. What was her goal? Getting into Cybil's bed? The idea was pleasant enough, though she knew deep down that it would be meaningless. The two of them had little in common. She didn't see them building a relationship. Not like what she and Dorry were building. Had been building.

Dorry wasn't here, though. And Cybil was. And she was warm and definitely willing. She had twice offered Marya a clear view of some very nice cleavage as she had leaned over and refreshed her drink, had caressed Marya's arm each time she took the glass.

They talked about Cybil's life. She was fresh out of a two-year relationship. Her partner, a closeted big-time Myrtle Beach lawyer, had decided that being with a man would be a better step on her way up the ladder to a political career. She had wanted to keep Cybil on the side, but Cybil had wanted none of that.

"I mean, what kind of woman does that? Hides the truth that way? I guess what they say about lawyers is true," she said.

"People never fail to amaze me," Marya answered.

"So, tell me about your ex," Cybil prompted. "What kind of business does she have?"

Marya looked at Cybil's expectant face and knew she couldn't talk about Dorry here. Not now. Not ever, probably. Maybe something else would work.

She reached across the small table and took Cybil's hand in hers. Pulling her to her feet, she led her toward the side of the bar and into the hallway outside the bathrooms. She saw a smile settle on Cybil's full lips as she realized where they were going. She pulled her into the surprisingly spacious ladies' room after her and into her arms.

"Sorry for the accommodations, my lady, but I find I am overcome with my immediate need for you." Marya pulled Cybil to her and kissed her long and hard, pushing her tongue into Cybil's mouth with passionate force. Cybil lurched against Marya and moaned, the sound a stimulus of incendiary proportions. Marya snaked a hand under Cybil's shirt, relishing the softness of her bare waist and hips. Spreading her other hand wide, she cupped Cybil's bottom through her nylon skirt, pressing their pelvises together.

Cybil brought up her arms and caressed Marya's neck as they kissed. Marya moved forward, shifting their bodies so that Cybil was against the wall, then brought her hands around to cup Cybil's small breasts in her palms.

Moaning again, Cybil lifted Marya's shirt from her trousers. Marya shifted to accommodate her...and the excruciating pain that followed almost brought her to her knees. For a brief moment she wondered if she were having a heart attack. Then she remembered her ribs. And Dorry. Reality came slamming back. It packed a powerful punch. She hissed in pain and backed away from Cybil, panting. "Oh my God, oh my God," she muttered. "What the fuck am I doing?"

"Marya? Are you okay?" Cybil asked, coming closer. Marya grasped both of Cybil's hands in hers.

"Look, don't hate me, Cybil. God knows you are hot and, oh yeah, I want you...but...but I gotta make things right with her, with Dorry. I just can't...please understand."

Cybil bit her bottom lip and nodded, eyes wide. "Sure, hon, I understand." She shrugged. "You gotta do what you gotta do."

Marya nodded and, letting go of Cybil, wrapped one arm protectively about her torso. Her other hand reached out and brushed Cybil's cheek gently. "I am sorry."

Cybil smiled. "Get on with you. Do what you have to do. If it doesn't work out, I'll still be here and we'll talk."

Marya nodded and limped painfully out of the bathroom and out of the Rainbow Spheres lounge.

***

The Fetch It Diner was just about empty by the time she got there. It was after the dinner rush and a young high school boy was busily busing the tables, probably so he could go home and play video games. Lisa greeted Marya from her usual perch behind the counter. Marya slid onto a low stool and asked for coffee. Lisa smiled and, placing a cup in front of her, filled it to the brim.

Marya wasn't sure what her next step needed to be, but she thought sobering up in the diner might be a good first step. She had toyed with the idea of going to her parents' house for the night but vetoed the idea quickly. She smelled more than a little like scotch and was broken all to hell. The fewer questions she had to answer for them, the better. She keenly remembered her mother's panicked call after Denton's body had been found.

The old codger sidled up to the counter and, with a grunt, settled onto the stool next to her. Ah, the trucker and somewhat annoying bearer of local lore. It was good to see him again. Leaning forward, she blew on her coffee and took a cautious sip.

"Well, look who's here," he said as he perused the menu.

"And a big hello to you. How was Maine?" She studied him. He looked the same. Only the clothing had changed. Today he was wearing faded blue jeans and a worn, untucked white button-down shirt.

"Cold. I pert near froze my ass off."

Marya laughed with difficulty, moaning a little as her ribs grated together.

"What the hell happened to you?" he asked, eyeing her with a worried glance.

"Man, you wouldn't believe it," she said, shaking her head.

"You havin' the usual, Kent?" Lisa asked. She waited expectantly on the other side of the counter.

"Yeah, Lisa, sounds good," he replied.

Lisa pulled out a cup and placed it in front of Kent. She filled it with coffee and pushed the sugar dispenser toward him, then moved off toward the kitchen to put in his order.

Kent poured a steady stream of sugar into his cup and spoke without looking at Marya. "Okay, I'm ready. Let's have it."

Marya hesitated only a second. She told him about getting the job at the paper. About the Dorry interview prank and then about the difficulty in getting the cottage. He shook his head now and again but didn't comment.

She then told him about Denton and about how he'd been murdered and how she and Dorry might be facing charges because of their taekwondo expertise. She wrapped up by telling him about Barnes, how he had picked a fight with her earlier that morning, breaking her ribs. And that she was debating whether or not to report him.

Kent gave a low whistle as Lisa placed his steaming plate of burger, fries and eggs in front of him.

"Sounds like he's your bad guy," he said. "You need to report that sucker."

"He sounds crazy as a June bug," Lisa said. "I think you need to report him too. You don't want to go to jail for something that maniac did. Let the police sort it out."

"Yeah, but will they believe me?" Marya asked.

"Seems to me you're wearing proof right there under that shirt," Lisa said as she slid a slice of apple pie in front of Marya.

Marya looked at the pie, then at Lisa. "What's this?"

"On the house," she said, swabbing the counter with a cloth. "Eat. You're skinny."

Marya laughed and looked at Kent.

He shrugged, chewing. "Better eat it," he said. "You don't want to mess with Lisa. You think those busted ribs hurt, but they ain't nothing compared to how she'll mess you up."

Lisa laughed and Marya and Kent joined in.

After a few moments of silent chewing, Kent spoke. "You know what you need to do, don't you?"

"What's that?" Marya responded.

"Trap the son of a bitch. Set up a sting and catch him in the act, so to speak."

Marya paused, a forkful of pie halfway to her mouth. "Oh my God, that is a great idea. He's got this big old jones for Dorry. I could use her as bait, get the police to wire her and then get him to admit to murdering Denton."

Lisa and Kent smiled at one another, satisfied. "See, problem solved," Kent said.

"I'd hug you if my ribs didn't hurt so badly," Marya responded.

Kent looked startled. "Oh, there's no need for all that," he said.

"You should go for it, Kent. She's skinny, but she's kinda cute," Lisa added as she moved to take the extra setups the busboy was handing her.

Marya regarded Kent as she chewed pie. "I dunno, you're not exactly my type," she said.

He laughed, the sound a low gurgle. "I know, I know. You like them Martians over there on Begaman Cove," he said quietly, grinning into his plate.

Marya laughed so hard she was afraid she might spew pie all over her new friend. She held her taped ribs tightly as laughter and tears poured forth in equal measure.

"Oh, lord, what did you do now, Kent," Lisa asked hands on her hips.

"Honey, hon…you need to calm down now," she told Marya. "No sense in busting them ribs up more than they are already."

"I'm okay," Marya gasped. "I gotta go tell the Martian about setting a trap to catch a bad guy."

She slid from the stool. "So, Kent, where you heading next?" she asked.

He sipped his coffee and sighed contentedly. "I'm home for the next week," he announced grandly. "First vacation I've had in eighteen months. Gonna be a good one too. Me and my forty-eight-inch flat screen."

Marya laughed and patted his shoulder.

"Lisa, thanks for the pie. It was delicious. And I'm gonna need it, I'm thinking. I know from experience, those Martians can be hard to deal with. They're hot-tempered, you know."

Kent snorted and Marya stepped out into the dusk.

CHAPTER THIRTY-THREE

All the windows at Dorry's house were dark. Marya checked her watch. Surely it was too early for Dorry to be in bed. Marya held her ribs and sighed. Well, at least she was there, judging from the fact that her truck was parked in the drive.

She knocked on the door but got no answer, so she tried the knob. Unlocked. She stepped inside, calling Dorry's name. She wasn't there, it seemed. Neither were Isabel's photos, Marya noted with a smile. She couldn't say she missed them. She hoped Dorry didn't either.

Five minutes later she was back in the living room and completely perplexed. She'd searched the entire house and

Dorry was nowhere to be found. Was she at the cottage maybe? Waiting for Marya to get home so they could fight some more? She left the house, pulling the front door closed behind her.

Marya decided to go home and deal with Dorry as best she could or with her aching ribs, whichever came first. She was opening the door to the Trooper and bracing herself for the increasingly painful climb into it, when she heard a faint cry. She strained her ears and heard it again, or thought she did, even over the sound of the ocean surf. It seemed to be coming from behind the house.

Gritting her teeth, Marya made her way over the uneven path that led back there. Sudden fear invaded her heart. What if someone had hurt Dorry…like Denton had been hurt. She slammed her terrified eyes shut, afraid what she might see in the adjoining woods.

The sound came again, from below her. She whirled toward the ocean. There! Beneath the back deck, in the enclosed swimming pool, was that movement that she was seeing? She drew closer, squinted her eyes to see. It was Dorry! And she was in trouble.

Moving as fast as her injured body allowed, Marya sped to the pool, shedding her wallet, phone and shoes as she went. She waded into the water, which deepened as she walked toward Dorry and was soon over her head. Treading water was agony. As quickly as she could, she dog-paddled to the ocean side of the pool and clung to its edge. Dorry was barely visible. Only the top of her silvered hair showed above the water…until the waves retreated back to the sea and the water receded a bit. Her face appeared then, just long enough for her to suck in a breath or two before the waves covered her again. Her eyes were frantic. Clearly, she'd become trapped somehow and couldn't free herself.

"Dorry? Dorry, what's holding you down?" Marya called when Dorry's face appeared the next time.

Dorry's lips were blue, evident even in the dimness beneath the deck, and her teeth chattered as she gasped out one word. "Rock."

Taking a deep breath, ignoring the pain that coursed through her torso, Marya dove below the surface. The salty seawater was murky and stung her eyes, but the crimson of Dorry's swimsuit served as a beacon that guided her downward. She saw with dismay that one of the huge boulders that defined the swimming area had rolled down on Dorry's leg, pinning her to the bottom of the rock wall.

Marya resurfaced and pulled close to Dorry. She waited for the waves to recede, then spoke loudly and clearly. "Help me roll the rock off. Now!"

She took another deep breath and dove down, pulling on Dorry's hands to help her go under. Their eyes met underwater for a brief moment, then together they struggled to shift the heavy boulder. Dorry was the first to let go, needing air. Marya surfaced alongside her.

"We'll get it, Dorry," she gasped, her hands cradling Dorry's wet, drawn face. "One more time, love, we can do this," she said, breaking off as a wave slapped at them. When it receded, Dorry nodded grimly and took a deep breath.

Marya dove down again, pulling Dorry with her. Again they struggled and this time, in a cloud of debris, the boulder rolled away, almost falling onto Marya's feet. She moved aside just in time. Alarmingly, the shift also released a frightening torrent of blood from Dorry's leg. Surfacing, Marya grabbed her and pulled her over to the shallows. Shit! Not only was her leg broken, bone was protruding from the skin. She pressed Dorry's hands to the wound, applying pressure to slow the bleeding.

"Christ! Hold on," she said. "I'll be right back."

Wearily, painfully, Marya pulled herself out of the pool and crawled along the grassy dunes behind the pool until her hands grasped her cell phone. She pressed the emergency button and told the dispatcher to send an ambulance right away, that Dorry was wounded and bleeding. Assured that help was coming, she hung up and slowly stood, bracing herself for the trip back to Dorry, who was intently watching, waiting to hear help was on the way. She waved and tried to smile. A sudden, tickling cough shook her and a gush of fluid spewed from her mouth and ran down her chin. She lifted her hands to catch it. They came back filled with bright red blood.

"What?" she gasped. She heard a strange crackling gurgle, then realized that she couldn't take in any air at all. Her eyes flew back to Dorry. She mouthed the words "I love you," hoping Dorry would see and understand. She took a step toward her, then another. And then her world went dark.

CHAPTER THIRTY-FOUR

The sounds penetrated first. Marya heard muffled conversation, odd beeping noises and what sounded like air hissing. She wanted very badly to speak, but her tongue was thick, like it was stuck to the roof of her mouth. She cracked her eyes open and saw pale daylight and a white ceiling.

"She's awake. Oh, thank goodness. Marya? Honey?"

Her mother's face materialized above her and then wobbled out of focus. She blinked her eyes and her mother's face stabilized.

"Richard? Is she okay?" Her mother watched her with concern.

"I'm sure she is, honey. These doctors know what they're doing."

Marya's father's face floated into her range of vision, and she blinked again, stabilizing him as well.

"Don't trouble yourself, pumpkin," her father said in a low, calm voice. "You're going to be fine. You had broken ribs that punctured and collapsed your lung." He brushed her hair back from her forehead.

"The EMT drew off air, though, and your lung re-inflated so you could breathe. The doctors did some tests after you got here and they say you're going to be fine," her mother added.

Marya had to smile. Her parents were actually sort of cute.

"Aww, she's smiling, Richard. That must mean she's feeling better." Her mother gazed at her lovingly, unshed tears brightening her eyes. Marya reached up a hand and clasped her mother's hand.

The next time Marya awakened she heard faint singing…a nursery rhyme in a voice she didn't recognize.

An unfamiliar male voice spoke. "I think she's awake, honey. Her eyes opened."

Marya turned her head haltingly toward the singing and found Carol sitting in the chair next to her bed. "Hey, girl," Carol said. "How are you feeling?"

Marya reached up and pulled the oxygen mask from her mouth. She cleared her throat, but even so, her voice was raspy and weak. "Good, good. What's that you have there?"

Carol smiled from ear to ear. She rose and brought her pink-blanketed bundle close to the bed. "I'd like you to meet Miss Alicia Blue Say. Alicia, Marya, Marya, Alicia."

Marya watched the rosy-skinned newborn squirm right out of her knitted cap and smiled, tears welling in her eyes. She reached and touched one of the tiny fingers and it wrapped around her finger with unexpected intensity. "Cute *and* strong," she whispered.

"We're just glad she's finally here," Buddy said, moving to stand behind his family. "And healthy."

"We're getting ready to head home, but we wanted to make sure you're okay. I expect a full report as soon as you recover, missy. I leave you guys alone for a few days and you go out and get all busted up. You know that's just *wrong*," she said.

They chatted a few more minutes, and then they left Marya alone. She replaced her oxygen mask, her thoughts flying to Dorry. Nobody had mentioned her. Fear swelled her heart. Had she lost her?

She shifted in her bed, making sure not to dislodge any of the various leads, and pulled herself into a sitting position. The room she was in was pleasant with a bay window that looked out beyond the highway and over the city of Schuyler Point. A silent television flickered on a nearby wall.

"Well, look at you," said a nurse as she strode into the room and studied Marya, arms akimbo. "I can see we're feeling better."

Marya smiled and pulled the mask loose again so she could talk.

"Much better but, boy, am I sore, all over," she whispered.

"Here, let me help you with that," the nurse said as she approached the bed and pulled the mask over Marya's head. She dismantled it, rolling up the tubing and tossing the mask in the waste bin. "You can talk normally now, hon. I know it's a little sore in there, but you don't need to be afraid of hurting anything. You're all patched up. We're basically just keeping an eye on you for now."

Marya started to pull out the tubing below her nose but the nurse stayed her hand. "Let's keep that nasal cannula in for just a little longer. A little bit of extra oxygen right now won't hurt a thing."

She poured water into a cup, added a bent straw and offered it to Marya. Marya dutifully took several sips. "Thank you."

The nurse took her pulse, listened to her chest sounds and her heartbeat and entered the information on her chart. "Let's get you up and to the facilities," she said, holding out a bent arm for support. Marya took it, pulled her legs around and placed her feet on the floor. The nurse unwrapped the plastic tubing on her oxygen supply to give her some slack and led her to the bathroom. She emerged, her bladder relieved and ready at last to relieve her mind. She steeled herself for the possibility of bad news.

"The woman who came in with me…do you know anything about her?" Marya asked as the nurse helped her back into bed. "Her name is Dorcas Wood."

The nurse laughed. "Oh, yes, we all know about Dorry. She's been driving us crazy, the doctors too, making sure you had the best of everything. She keeps going around telling everyone on the ortho floor what a hero you are and how you saved her life. She's been up here every day in her wheelchair, checking on you."

The nurse grinned at Marya. "And I bet there's not one single patient on this cardio floor who doesn't know what a hero you are too."

Marya smiled, relief and love filling her completely. Dorry was okay. That's all she needed to know.

CHAPTER THIRTY-FIVE

Marya walked over and hunkered down behind a thick stand of pine. Inspector March was already there. The cell he planned to use to call the backup cars was clasped in his hand.

"So, how much longer?" he asked, his voice tight with anxiety.

She glanced at her watch, holding it up to improve visibility in the gathering dusk. "Another fifteen minutes. Dorry set the meeting for nine."

"He knows she's alone?"

"Yep, she asked him if he would mind moving a few boxes for her because no one else was available."

"Ahh," March said. "Smart move."

"Yeah, I thought so," she answered. It had taken two weeks to convince the sheriff, first, that he should consider Barnes a prime suspect in Denton's death and, second, that Dorry, even in a full leg cast and wheelchair, was more than capable of handling anything untoward that might crop up. They'd imagined every contingency, developing not only a Plan B, but a Plan C and a Plan D as well. They'd set the best trap for him that they could. They just had to wait now for him to walk into it.

She started in alarm as a uniformed figure approached the house from the access road where a parked cruiser was barely visible.

"What the…! Hey, March, there's a…" she began just as his cell vibrated.

"Yeah," March answered it. "Okay, got it."

He turned toward her. "It's just Thomas. He's going down below, where he can be available for immediate support."

"He won't push it, will he?" she asked. That's all they needed, some hotheaded deputy going off half-cocked and tipping the guy off. Especially since Barnes *was* his taekwondo master.

"I don't think so. Gennis says he gave him strict orders. He's just going to wait there until they signal the officers to enter."

Marya relaxed, but only slightly, and nodded to show she understood. They waited.

***

Inside the house, Dorry waited as well. She was trying hard to even out her breathing and slow the beat of her anxious heart. As a taekwondo master, she should have been able to do so easily, but she wasn't feeling very masterly at the moment. She sighed and squirmed in the wheelchair. To top everything off, her broken leg was itching inside the cast. She tapped the outside of it absently with one fingertip as she peered out the side window.

Could Barnes have killed Denny? It was hard for her to fathom. Sure, he had some kind of weird obsession for her, but killing Denny would only alienate her. Surely he had to realize that.

"Stop tapping, Dorry," Marya said in her ear. "It's making us crazy over here."

Dorry let out a short bark of laughter but stopped her mindless drumming. It wasn't helping the itch anyway. She glanced at the wall clock. It was time.

Automobile lights appeared at the top of Dorry's drive.

"Here we go," she whispered.

"We see it," Marya replied. "Hang tough. We've got your back and Thomas is downstairs. You okay?"

"I'm okay," Dorry said softly, her heart thrilling at the caring concern in Marya's voice.

Dorry rolled herself to the rear of the room, so her back would be to the wall. She folded her hands together and willed herself into calmness. *What will be will be*, she thought repeatedly. *What will be will be*.

When Barnes knocked and entered, Dorry was surprised to see flowers in his hands, beautiful crimson roses bound with a wide, deep blue ribbon. He smiled at her and closed the door.

"Hello, Dorry," he said. "How are you doing?"

"I'm okay," she responded. "What's this then?" She indicated the flowers.

"They're for you." He placed them in her lap, then stepped back and lowered his head. "It means a lot to me that you asked me over. I...I've been hoping you would."

Dorry grunted, the smell of roses filling her head. "You have, huh?"

"Yes." He paused as if mulling over what to say. "I know the restraining order says I shouldn't be here without your permission. So it meant a lot to me that you asked me over to help you out." He paused as if uncertain what to say next. "And I'm so sorry you got hurt."

"Thank you, Freddy. I'm not sure what happened, but we were friends once." Dorry's voice was calm, belying the feelings roiling inside her.

A silence fell between them. After a few moments, Barnes spoke. "You know…as a team we could be very powerful."

Dorry indicated the sofa. "Sit and tell me what you mean."

Barnes perched on the edge of the sofa, and Dorry breathed a small sigh of relief. She knew she had the skills necessary to protect herself, but having him standing over her had been intimidating.

"I've been thinking about this ever since that time in North Carolina, since that moment we had. About how… intense…we could be together. You know, if we…if I just… took a little of your essence. Your tiger essence…" he faltered. "You don't understand, I know, but…but think about it…"

Dorry was bewildered. "Think about what, Fred? What moment in North Carolina?"

Barnes closed his eyes, sadness creasing his features. "The competition. Raleigh. You took me down in round one. I saw it there for just a moment, in just that instance, that tiger essence in your eyes. I was shamed, yes, completely, but I realized, in that shame, that this day would come. That one day we would merge forces and be one powerful force to be reckoned with. That our two schools would become one."

Dorry was becoming aggravated. "Freddy, what are you talking about? What does that have to do with Denny?" She paused as she heard Marya's warning hiss in her ear.

Barnes studied Dorry as if she were the one who had lost her mind. "Denny? Denton, your brother-in-law? What does he have to do with us? Didn't he die?"

In for a penny, in for a pound. Dorry ignored the cautioning voice in her ear. "Exactly. And I believe you are responsible." Her hands moved from the roses and gripped the rubber wheels of the chair.

Barnes fell quiet, head tilted as though working math sums in his head. His eyes stared blankly at Dorry. "I'm not sure I understand what you mean," he said.

"This is getting tedious," muttered Dallas, stepping into the room. Swinging her arm wide, she brought the heavy candlestick in her hand down on Barnes's head, connecting with a sickening, awful, cracking noise.

"Dallas, what the hell!" Dorry tried to leap to her feet, forgetting about her broken leg, and ended up collapsing in a heap next to Barnes's body on the floor. His eyes were open and fixed. Dorry's heart clenched in sadness at the sight. In her ear, she heard Marya shouting, "It's not him, it's not him!" Working out ways to keep Dallas busy until the police could arrive, she used her arms to pull herself into a semi-sitting position.

"Now, Dallas," she began, speaking slowly and carefully. "I don't know what you're up to but I think you'd better rethink it." She pushed rose stems and petals aside, making sure her hands would be able to maneuver her body as needed and scanning the room, trying to determine where the social editor had moved to.

Dallas chuckled. The sound drew Dorry's gaze to the bar. She was leaning against it, panting from the exertion and excitement of hitting Barnes. The bloodied candlestick still dangled from one gloved hand. "Rethink. Rethink? That's all I've done for twenty-odd years is think. Think about why she never let me talk to him, that bitch. She let him think his precious Francie was his only child and here was my poor baby, left all alone with no daddy. Boys need a daddy, don't they?"

She moved closer and shook the candlestick at Dorry. "She is one iron-clad bitch, that one is," she said. "I'm sure Nicky regrets that choice."

"Oh my God, Mama. What have you done?" Thomas entered the room from the back hallway. "What have you done?"

"Shoot her, boy. Shoot her quickly. A killing shot. Say the bitch killed him, then came at you. Hurry now. I'll meet you at home." Dallas threw the candlestick down and turned toward the back of the house.

A low laugh rumbled in Dorry's chest, then emerged to rule the night. Thomas and Dallas turned to her, shame written on one face, confusion on the other.

"Go ahead, Thomas, tell her," Dorry said.

Twin high-beam lights roved across the ceiling and around the room. Thomas danced nervously in place, a low moan issuing from his lips.

Dallas glanced at the approaching car lights, then slipped into the darkness of the hallway. "Tell me at home later," she said as she fled. "Shoot her, shoot her now!"

Before he could act, the front door burst open and Inspector March, Marya and three deputies rushed inside. A shrieking cacophony broke out in the back of the house, growing louder and more vile as Sheriff Gennis marched Dallas back into the room. She was trying to wriggle free, all the while screaming at him, but he had her arms securely pinned behind her.

Marya raced to Dorry's side and hunkered down next to her. "Oh God, are you okay? Okay? Are you? Really?" Marya's words were a jumble of ceaseless worry.

Dorry grabbed Marya's fluttering hands to still them. She pulled her close and looked into Marya's eyes. "Yes, I am fine. Calm down now. Breathe."

Marya threw her arms around Dorry's neck and buried her face in it, missing the abrupt entrance of Isabel and the tall man in a khaki uniform who was with her.

Isabel paused in the doorway, taken aback by Marya and Dorry's embrace and then by the sight of Barnes's body on the floor. The officer crouched beside him, searching for a pulse, was shaking his head.

Isabel lifted a hand to her open mouth. "Oh, Dorry. What has happened?" she gasped.

At the sound of her voice, Marya pulled out of the embrace, but she stayed close, moving just enough to allow two of the deputies to lift Dorry back into her chair. Once she was settled in it, she stood behind the wheelchair, a possessive hand on the back of it, but itching to rest it on Dorry's shoulder instead.

"It was Dallas," Dorry replied dully. "Dallas. She was the one. Though how she…"

Isabel sighed. "Thomas, that's how. Her son. And… Nicky's."

Marya looked from Isabel to Thomas. "What? Dallas had a son? And with…with Nicholas?"

"But they were too good to own up to it, weren't they?" Dallas growled from across the room. "I thought maybe after Dorry let Francie die, Nicky would be glad to have his son but, oh no," she sneered. "This bitch wouldn't let me talk to him even then."

Nicholas, who turned out to be Isabel's tall companion, stepped behind his wife and rested his hands on her shoulders. "Dallas, you know Isabel was just looking out for me. After Francie died, I couldn't think about anything, much less something as important as this."

"But we could have been a family, Nicky," Dallas cajoled. "I sent you so many letters…I tried to call. She just…"

Nicholas moved from Isabel to Thomas, who was standing in handcuffs, his head drooping sullenly. "I'm so sorry, Thomas. I…I never knew."

"You never wanted to know," Thomas replied quietly. "Now, it doesn't even matter. I never cared anyway. I was happy with just Mama."

"Look, break this up," Inspector March said. "All of you need to come to the station for statements. We'll get to the bottom of things there."

"Wait," Dorry said, her authoritative voice ringing throughout the room. "I have to know…Which of you killed Denny and why?"

Silence fell and persisted for a long beat.

"He was nosing around," Thomas said finally. "Mama saw what he was printing out at work…my birth certificate… and she called me. He was bringing it to you, even though the father was listed as Nick Cross. I guess he put two and two together. We had to get it back from him so no one would know about me and Mama. So we hid him. And then he tried to get away, when I brought him food. I swear…it was an accident. He was an old man…so old and…"

"Shut up, Thomas," Dallas hissed. "Hush right this instant!"

"I agree," said Sheriff Gennis. "Thomas Cross, you are under arrest for the murder of Denton Hyde. You have the right to remain silent. Anything you say or do can and will be held against you in a court of law. You have the right to speak to an attorney and if you cannot afford an attorney, one will be appointed for you…Do you understand these rights?"

Thomas nodded and he and his mother were escorted to the waiting cruiser. Isabel and Nicholas were led out by Inspector March. He paused to look back at Dorry and Marya. "You'll be along then?"

CHAPTER THIRTY-SIX

Marya held Dorry's hand. They'd been through it, no doubt about that. Into the crucible and out again. Together.

"I still can't believe it," she said. "Imagine sweet little Dallas raising a monster like that."

She rose slowly, lifting Dorry's cup and moving to the counter to get more coffee for them both. They were commiserating over breakfast in Dorry's small, tidy kitchen, still reeling from the shock of the previous day.

Dorry leaned back in her wheelchair. "I had my doubts about her. She's not so sweet."

"Obviously," Marya said, smiling. "I'm glad you're okay, Dorry," she added softly. "I was really worried for a while there."

"Me too, love. Worried about both of us." She laughed softly, ruefully.

"So let me get this straight. Dallas was with Nicholas before Isabel and got pregnant with Thomas."

Dorry nodded. "Yes. But it was a one-time thing. They never really had a relationship."

"Nicholas never knew about the baby?"

"Right."

"Then Isabel got pregnant with Francie?"

"Correct."

"So Thomas and Francie have the same father."

Again a nod. "Yes."

"So why didn't Isabel tell Nicholas? He had a right to know."

Dorry sighed, becoming very interested in her coffee. "Isabel told me that it was the way Dallas approached her. She acted entitled...and she was very bitter because Nicky had left her for Isabel. Even so, Isabel did try to help. Felt sorry for her being left alone with a toddler so she started sending her some money each month."

"And she didn't tell Nicholas? How did she hide that?"

Dorry shrugged. "He was traveling, assigned to various short stations, and Isabel had just realized she was pregnant right about that time. When Dallas approached her, I think she was afraid Nicky would leave her and go back to Dallas."

"Would he have?"

"Good question. I doubt it. He was so wrapped up in Francie and Isabel but...he has a massive sense of duty. That would have played a powerful role."

Marya tapped a forefinger on her chin. "Being a military man and all."

"Yes." Dorry sat back. "So she sent money, over and over again, each month. But..." She sighed and shifted in her seat. "Dallas had started going off the deep end. Isabel set up a post office box because she didn't want Dallas to know where they lived after they left Germany and moved to Bethesda. Dallas inundated the box with photocopies. Most were of bills. Expenses. Even the most mundane… groceries even. She wanted Isabel and Nicholas to pay for them. Expected them to pay."

"Wow," she said quietly.

"I know," she agreed. "These bills would be interspersed with vitriolic letters of hatred and crazy demands. Isabel said she ignored most of them and just sent her regular monthly cash. This went on for years."

"I'd say so," she interjected, "like twenty-five."

Dorry nodded and drained her cup. "Yes. Oddly enough."

Silence grew between them. Marya was mulling over the situation. A sudden thought occurred. "And you knew all of this the whole time? Why didn't you tell me?"

Dorry eyed her quizzically. "Oh no, honey. I never knew any of it. Not until the day of the fund-raiser."

"She kept the secret, even from you, for all those years?" She was amazed.

"Yes." Dorry's voice softened. "Even from me."

"I'm curious. Why didn't Dallas go through the military?"

"Well, Isabel said she did," Dorry replied as she studied Marya's lips. "But he's an officer and, because of the crazy way she was acting, I believe they just assumed she was some crackpot trying to ruin him and get him in trouble with his wife."

"Not surprising," she added sullenly. "The service is pretty much a good old boys network. So what did Isabel say, when she told you about all this?"

"That she was going to tell Nicky and be done with it. That's why they were here. Are here. So Nicky could meet Thomas."

"Thomas. He killed Denton, right?"

"Right."

"And hung the dead birds in the cottage?"

"Yes and wrecked my office too. Seems Thomas paid Rob to leave the back door unlocked."

Marya eyed Dorry with one eyebrow raised.

"I know," Dorry said with a scowl. "I'm sorry."

Marya smiled to show there were no hard feelings. "I bet Dallas erased Denton's computer files because he had some kind of proof in there about Thomas's birth."

"I bet," Dorry agreed.

"But what about your bracelet? How did it get in my bed? And why?" She paused, one finger to her chin. "Oh my God, Thomas planted it in my room while I was busy with Inspector March. To implicate both of us. He must have gotten it from Dallas."

"Or from my house. I wonder why he didn't he bring it to the Inspector's attention," Dorry added.

Marya shrugged. "Maybe he just wanted to spook me, make me believe you were guilty."

"Did it work?" Dorry was watching her closely.

"Almost," Marya admitted. "And all this time we assumed it was Barnes."

"Why would we suspect Thomas?" Dorry asked. "Freddy seemed a much more likely suspect. Look at the weird way he was acting."

Marya looked down at her hands. "Despite what he did to me, I feel badly about what happened to him. What Dallas did. I also hate that she caused that whole Francie thing."

Dorry looked out the window at the forested, sloping hill behind her house. "I do too, Marya, I do too."

***

Later that morning there was a knock at the door. It was Isabel.

"Hello, Marya," she said, extending her hand. "I don't think we've met formally. I'm Isabel Rose."

Marya took the hand, finding it soft and delicate in texture. "Hello, Isabel. It's good to finally meet you."

Marya ushered her in and took her to the screened back porch where Dorry rested, her injured leg propped on pillows. Dorry looked up in surprise. When she saw Isabel, her eyes flew to Marya as if in apology.

"I'll make some iced tea," Marya said as she gestured for Isabel to have a seat on the sofa next to Dorry.

In the kitchen, Marya put the kettle on, then leaned her head back against the refrigerator and stared at the ceiling. Would she lose Dorry now?

Scenarios populated her imagination. Had Nicholas left Isabel because she didn't tell him about Thomas? Was Isabel free and, if so, could she and Dorry take up a life together after all these years? Or would Isabel's visit here devastate Dorry? Leave her unfulfilled and yearning?

How could Marya compete?

Moments later, as she carried the tray of iced tea onto the porch, she saw Isabel rise and embrace Dorry. She breezed past Marya, thanking her for the tea, which she had to forego because Nicholas was waiting.

"I know you two will be very happy," she said, looking into Marya's eyes, one hand on her shoulder. "You are good for one another."

Marya watched the empty doorway, the tray growing ever heavier in her hands. She finally placed it on the small table next to Dorry and turned to the woman she loved.

"Is everything okay?" she asked.

"We talked about old loves," said Dorry. She gazed into Marya's eyes. "And how old loves make way for new loves."

Marya moved closer, a bee drawn in by the sweet nectar of Dorry's loving gaze. "How about it, Marya? Will you be my new love? My last love?"

Marya pressed her lips to Dorry's and knew that she had found her true home at last. "Yes, my darling. I am your forever love."

Bella Books, Inc.

Women. Books. Even Better Together.

P.O. Box 10543

Tallahassee, FL 32302

Phone: 800-729-4992

www.bellabooks.com